"I'm not the bad guy.
I don't know why you're on this plane."

Her dark eyes studied his, looking for the truth in his words.

"The name's Connor Jacobson, by the way."

"Maya," she said. She tugged a strand of her beautiful dark hair away from her face, revealing the shadows under her eyes.

"Maya?" he asked, hoping for a little more.

That's all she would give. It was enough for now.

Connor leaned forward, his elbows on his knees. "I have a feeling, Maya, that you might know more about what's going on than me. So why don't you spill."

He wished he knew how to completely convince her he wasn't involved in her kidnapping, but that was only one of the many problems her presence on the plane presented.

The woman had been traumatized, and Connor would give her the space she needed for as long as he could, before he pressed her for information.

He glanced at his watch. She had half an hour.

Books by Elizabeth Goddard

Love Inspired Suspense

Freezing Point
Treacherous Skies

ELIZABETH GODDARD

is a seventh-generation Texan who grew up in a small oil town in East Texas, surrounded by Christian family and friends. Becoming a writer of Christian fiction was a natural outcome of her love of reading, fueled by a strong faith.

Elizabeth attended the University of North Texas where she received her degree in computer science. She spent the next seven years working in high-level sales for a software company located in Dallas, traveling throughout the United States and Canada as part of the job. At twenty-five, she finally met the man of her dreams and married him a few short weeks later. When she had her first child, she moved back to East Texas with her husband and daughter and worked for a pharmaceutical company. But then, more children came along and it was time to focus on family. Elizabeth loves that she gets to do her favorite things every day—read, write novels, stay at home with her four precious children, and work with her adoring husband in ministry.

ELIZABETH GODDARD

TREACHEROUS
SKIES

Recycling programs
for this product may
not exist in your area.

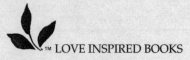 ™ LOVE INSPIRED BOOKS

ISBN-13: 978-0-373-44519-6

TREACHEROUS SKIES

www.LoveInspiredBooks.com

Printed in U.S.A.

God made him who had no sin to be sin for us,
so that in him we might become
the righteousness of God.
—*2 Corinthians* 5:21

Dedicated to my loving husband, Dan. Always.

Acknowledgments

Let me express my deepest gratitude
to two extraordinary pilots, Steve Ferrell
and Rodney Henderson, for their willingness
to answer my many questions with detailed
accounts of how things work, and for reading
through my scenes and offering suggestions and
corrections. I couldn't have written this story
without the assistance of these two dedicated and
experienced pilots. You guys are real heroes!

ONE

Belize City, Belize

Maya Carpenter glanced around the crowd in the Blue Moon Café, searching for her father, a man she hadn't seen since she was five years old. A man wanted in ten countries, including this one.

Though uncertain she'd recognize him, he'd said he would know her. A glance at her watch told her he was already twenty minutes late. This wasn't the type of circumstance that allowed for tardiness.

Something was wrong.

That meant he probably wasn't going to show. She'd spent a lifetime trying to escape her heritage, but he'd sounded so sincere on the phone two weeks ago—the first contact since she was five—when he shared that he was terminally ill and wanted to see her one last time.

In that moment, he'd been convincing, and how could anyone deny their father a dying wish? She hadn't even realized it until his call, but she needed closure. Maya had finally agreed, but now?

Doubts suffused her to the core.

She scraped her bag from the chair as she stood and rushed from the table in search of the door. She weaved her way through the dining patrons and dodged the tray-toting waiters until she spotted the exit.

Had she walked into some sort of trap?

But this was her *father*. He'd supported her mother fleeing to the U.S. from Colombia with Maya after the kidnapping that almost cost her life. He'd never harmed her other than with his poor career choice.

Outside the Blue Moon Café, she found the sidewalk rimming the street and hurried to the parking lot.

A black sedan edged to the curb next to her and she picked up her pace. The door opened and a man in a suit stepped out and into her path. She tried to skirt around him, but he gently grabbed her arm.

"Señorita Carpenter, your father," he said, his Spanish accent thick, and gestured to the inside of the vehicle.

She leaned forward to peer inside the four-door sedan and there, sitting on the far side in the shadows of the backseat, was Colombian drug lord Eduardo Ramirez. At least, she supposed it was him, though she couldn't really remember his face, and he would have changed after all these years, as had she.

Maya's pulse thrummed in her ears and dizziness swept over her.

He stretched his hand toward her, inviting her in. Either she was about to fill a huge hole in a lifetime of hurt and bring closure, or she was the biggest fool that ever lived.

She slid into the seat next to him, and the man on the sidewalk shut the door.

"Papá?" Uncertainty ripped through her as the endearment fell flat.

"Maya, my precious girl. It's been far too long since I've seen you." The man's laugh was warm and friendly, yet laced with menace. It was definitely not her father's but somehow familiar. "But no, I'm your father's worst nightmare."

"It's now or never."

Connor Jacobson peeled the catering van from his hiding place in the thick forest a safe distance from the airstrip where he and his brother Jake had remained undetected.

Throughout the morning, he'd watched the Learjet for the telltale signs it was being prepped to leave the country—pretending to deliver a catered lunch in order to gain access to the jet wouldn't work otherwise.

While he watched, the jet had been refueled and though he hoped to see someone perform a preflight check, getting by those armed guards would be tricky. Adding a couple of pilots into the mix might kill the plan completely. Connor didn't want anyone to get hurt, and that meant he'd have to move fast.

Troy McDaniels of Genesis Air Holdings, an aviation leasing company, had hired Connor to recover the Learjet, making him a Learjet repo man, of sorts.

At least for today.

The men with guns complicated what he'd been led to believe would be the simple recovery of a sleek, private Learjet costing in the millions.

People weren't usually willing to give up their expensive toys and apparently would go as far as hiding them, but employing a security detail to protect property that no longer belonged to them seemed a little extreme.

This was some serious on-the-job-training for Connor's first time, because Troy hadn't said anything about Uzi-toting guards. But Troy *had* suggested Connor consider using the element of surprise. Now he knew why.

The van bumped over the road, grating at Connor's already agitated mood. They hadn't bargained for this. If only he had more than two days to think this through, but he'd been informed that after that time the jet would be out of the country and more difficult to extract.

For the same reason, he'd wait to file a flight plan, and grab his clearance after takeoff. If someone got wind of his plans, the Learjet was as good as gone, taking his hopes for a future with it.

Gunning the van, he tossed a grin Jake's way, hoping to invigorate his brother, his face now a few shades lighter.

"I've come to appreciate that your charm has its advantages."

Jake had convinced a woman to let him use her catering truck for the morning, though some extra cash had been required to seal the deal. She'd been given the necessary directions about where to find her vehicle later in the day. That is, if everything went as planned.

Now that he'd seen just how remote this airstrip was, he wasn't sure they'd paid her enough.

"You're sure a plate of cupcakes is going to convince them?" Jake gripped the overhead handle as Connor floored it over the rutted road to the airfield. "I'd think that caviar would be more in line with what they're expecting."

"Relax. There are five plates of sandwiches that, for all they know, were made special for the rich and unscrupulous. They won't be able to tell the sandwiches are nothing more than tuna. Those will convince them if they question us, which they won't, and it only takes one platter to get us on the plane. Once we're on, there's nothing they can do unless they want to shoot holes in the plane. I doubt they've been given that authority."

Or at least he hoped they hadn't. At the moment, hope was all he had.

From the corner of his eye, Connor could tell that while his brother had agreed to come along at first, now he was losing his nerve—and fast. Connor had invited him for one reason—he needed a copilot to fly the jet and Jake was an experienced commercial pilot for Journey Airlines. Connor had dragged his brother away the day before he was to leave for his vacation in Hawaii. His only regret at the moment was potentially putting his brother in harm's way.

"Jake, we're posing as caterers. If they won't let us on, we'll think of something else. They're not going to shoot us for bringing cupcakes. Once we're on the plane, we shut the door and take off. Got it?"

"Got it." His brother shifted in his seat, appearing to grab on to the idea as though his life depended on it.

It just might.

Connor's pulse raced in his ears as he drove around the lone hangar on the remote airstrip. One of the guards came into view. The other must have disappeared into the hangar.

Connor parked the van near the door to the jet where the guard eyed them. Fortunately, he hadn't assumed an aggressive posture that signaled suspicion, and a quick glimpse told Connor the other one wasn't on his way back. Amazing what a van decorated in the flowering script of a catering business could do.

"Wipe your palms, buddy." Connor laughed as he spoke to Jake, hoping the guard standing like a sentinel next to the bird would see that he and Jake were good ole boys just doing their job.

Connor wondered if they were expecting the jet to be repossessed or if they were protecting the plane for another reason. If the lessee was mixed up in something requiring armed guards, it was none of Connor's business. He was just there for the plane.

When Connor stepped from the vehicle, he strode around the front of the van to speak with the dark-haired sentry. Connor tugged a slip of paper from his pocket and stared at it as though he needed confirmation.

"We're here to deliver food to a jet on this strip, and the N-number matches. Never mind there's only two jets here and this one is the only white Learjet with black-and-gold stripes." Connor laughed, but the guard didn't crack a smile.

He held out a pink-frosted cupcake with red sprinkles. "I was afraid we'd be late. You hungry?" he asked.

The guard eyed the cupcake then glanced over at the hangar. Finally he shook his head. "No."

Connor got the sense the guy wanted the cupcake, but thought better of it. Good. The man believed the story. "Suit yourself."

Jake got out of the vehicle, his demeanor a little too cautious for Connor, but then again, the guns should intimidate any normal person. He slapped his brother on the back and slid the side of the van door open to reveal the food. Each of them grabbed a tray.

The guard slid his key into the Learjet door, unlocked and tugged down the steps, then lifted the top section for them. Jake hopped up the three short steps into the jet and then made a show of entering the cabin to deposit the plate after which he would slip into the cockpit where he would begin the start-up sequence. It would take thirty seconds for each of the engines to start, but they only needed one to taxi the jet down the runway, putting distance between them and the guards, and they could start the other engine during the taxi.

Connor handed off one of the two plates to the guard, buying a little time. The guard hesitated at first then finally took the plate.

"Help yourself. There's an extra plate anyway." He gestured to the van. "Drinks are in the van."

He hopped up the steps and entered the jet, joining his brother. They had no more than ten seconds, if that, before the distracted guard noticed he'd been outmaneuvered.

When Connor spotted the guard heading to the hangar with the plate of cupcakes, he tugged the steps closed and shut them inside the jet.

Jake began the start-up sequence, and Connor watched the hangar through the small window.

Fifteen seconds and counting.

The guards appeared at the hangar entrance and launched toward them, holding their weapons in the air.

"Jake. Get this thing moving."

Connor couldn't lock the guards out, so he secured the door by holding the handle in place. They would be on him in seconds.

The door shook as the two gun-toting men tried to open it. They pounded on it, spewing curses.

The first engine fired up. Jake began taxiing the jet. The guards banged harder against the door.

Were they going to shoot? Connor held his breath and sent up a silent prayer.

Jake increased their speed until the guards could no longer keep up.

Connor dropped into the pale leather captain's chair in the cockpit next to his brother. The first engine had reached the ten percent mark, and Connor brought number-two thrust lever forward.

Gunfire pinged the fuselage, sounding like the last

couple of kernels of popcorn in the microwave. He hoped the bullets didn't pierce the exterior.

"I thought you said they wouldn't shoot?" In the close quarters of the cockpit, Jake's glare felt more like a death threat.

"I guess they figure they're in big trouble for losing the plane over a plate of cupcakes." Connor thought that would make his brother laugh, but Jake's expression remained solemn.

The Lear increased speed down the runway until they lifted into the air. Connor's elation soared with the jet, his relief palpable. "Now that we're airborne, get us clearance so we can start climbing to altitude."

Communications complete, they continued increasing altitude. Heart knocking against his rib cage, Connor felt more alive than he had in months. They had actually succeeded.

He released a long sigh, his adrenaline-powered energy expended for the moment. "We made it."

"Are you saying you had any doubt? Because you sure went out of your way to convince me it would be a piece of cupcake." Jake laughed, his face finally relaxing. "I can't believe I survived that."

"Yeah, I guess I still owe you, then."

"I'm not sure you can afford to repay me."

"That bad, huh?"

"With the time you spent in Iraq getting shot down, and then flying those test planes, I'd say you're accustomed to facing death on a daily basis. Me? I enjoy life too much."

"Sorry about that. This wasn't exactly what I imagined we'd face, either."

In repossessing the jet, he'd fully expected to walk into the airport, present the required documentation—

insurance, lease termination, power of attorney, the works—then file a new flight plan and fly the plane out. That was before he and his copilot brother had discovered the Learjet had been moved to a private, uncontrolled airfield an hour and a half drive from the airport in Belize City.

That also was before they'd seen the two armed men lurking near the jet as though they were expecting a hostile takeover. But it didn't matter anymore. He and Jake had the jet now, and Connor was on his way to getting his life back on track.

While serving as a fighter pilot, he'd crashed and burned once too often, and the Flying Evaluation Board had deemed him unable to fly safely. He'd lost his wings and served out the rest of his term as an Air Liaison Officer. Then as a test pilot, crash and burn had officially become his M.O. or *modus operandi*.

Though most people didn't consider an ex-fighter pilot anything but a hero, Connor couldn't help but think of himself as a loser. He'd wanted to be an Air Force hero like his dad, like his grandfather, but he'd failed miserably. Maybe if he switched gears and gave up the risky flying jobs altogether, he wouldn't be the loser of the family anymore. He'd be able to get back on speaking terms with Reg, his older, overachieving brother.

If he'd gotten on track sooner, then maybe…Connor would still be engaged.

Retrieving the jet would secure him the funds he needed to buy the aeronautical business that serviced the airport, making him an FBO, or fixed-based operator, and keeping him firmly planted on the ground.

Too bad the only way to get those funds had been another risky job. Too bad he had the feeling that settling down wouldn't be as easy as he thought.

Wanting to shake the negative thoughts, Connor stood to shrug out of his jacket. A loud bang resounded from the back of the cabin. Stunned silence passed between Connor and Jake.

"I'll check it out," Connor said.

Dread sliced through him as he exited the cockpit. He hadn't even considered searching the plane first. He'd assumed Jake would have at least taken a cursory glance in the lavatory since he was the first one on. But then again they hadn't exactly had time for anything besides a quick escape.

As he strode down the aisle he took in the extravagantly furnished and spacious cabin. Rich, supple leather covered the reclining seats and walls, and an elegant wood veneer, the cabinets and accent trim.

The pounding continued and he searched the compartments for a weapon. It was reasonable to expect a person that would hire security with Uzis would also store a weapon for personal protection somewhere on this rig. Connor almost wished he'd smuggled his nine millimeter into Belize with him. It hadn't seemed worth the risk, but he hadn't known then what he knew now.

"Connor," Jake called from the cockpit.

He spun around. Jake dangled a firearm from the trigger guard. "Found it under the seat."

Connor made his way back to retrieve the gun. Once he held the nine millimeter in his hands he made sure a few rounds were chambered.

Glock 'n' roll.

Jake cleared his throat. "You know what happens when we shoot guns on planes, right?"

His brother worried too much. Though using a firearm in a pressurized cabin wasn't the smartest thing, it wasn't as if one bullet hole—or even several—in the fuselage would cause an explosive decompression.

Maybe just a slow pressure leak. Before Connor could return the sarcasm, the knocking grew louder.

Connor held his weapon at the ready and swallowed—the last thing he needed was a situation in which he was forced to actually use the gun in his hands.

He opened the door.

Terrified, honey almond eyes stared back at him, the woman's mouth smothered with duct tape.

TWO

Maya stared down the barrel of a weapon aimed straight at her.

Her bravado bled out of her.

No, not like this!

She crumpled under the threat of a bullet to the head and pleaded with her eyes, while trying to force her muffled pleas through the duct tape. The man behind the gun narrowed his gaze as she begged with hers.

When he moved in, a sudden surge of desperation exploded inside her. Sitting back in the lavatory, she seized what she saw as her last chance of survival and kicked him in the face, slamming her tethered heels into his jaw.

The force of her kick propelled him against the wall opposite the door. Maya stood, prepared to fight her way out. Though stunned, he recovered too quickly.

He moved his jaw in an exaggerated way, as though testing the damage, but stood prepared, regarding her with caution.

"Listen, I'm not the bad guy here." He put the gun away.

How did she expect her to believe that when he was on a plane headed to Bogotá, a kidnapped woman in tow?

She screamed, the sound bursting through her head, and charged him.

He dodged, and she slammed into the wall. Raging pain burned through her shoulder, and though she tried to remain standing, turbulence and dizziness pushed her to the floor, where she lay heaving. Okay. So she couldn't fight her way out of this with brawn; she'd have to use her brain—if only she hadn't listened to her heart when her father called.

Strong arms cradled her, then lifted her from the floor. "It looks like you've been through the wringer, but I promise I had nothing to do with it."

Maya started to buck in protest, despite the sincerity she heard in his voice.

"Shh." He placed her gently into one of eight comfortable leather seats in a lavishly decorated cabin.

"If you'll calm down long enough for me to remove the tape and the plastic ties, then maybe we can figure out what's going on."

Remaining in the cockpit, the other pilot leaned over in his seat to eye the situation. Maya glared at the man who stood over her, wishing her eyes were stilettos. Maybe she could stab him with her stare.

The woman could slice through him with the look she gave. Connor took a step back and shrugged, his heart pounding in rhythm with his jaw at this new development.

"Do you want me to set you free, or should I stuff you back in the lavatory?" Ouch. He cringed at his harsh tone.

Her body language wasn't very encouraging, and he felt cruel for not immediately cutting her free. But she could pose a threat. At the moment, he didn't have a clue what he was dealing with.

For a split second, he considered turning the plane around and giving her back. Finding an abducted woman inside the airplane he was repossessing was above his pay scale, or at least was another left-out detail for which he'd been unprepared. Regardless, he didn't consider turning back to face submachine guns an option.

She stared up at him, her eyes filled with a mixture of confusion, fear and anger.

Connor sighed. "Look, I'm sorry. I shouldn't have said that, but just calm down. I'm not going to hurt you." He moved in, approaching her slowly as though she might bite if he moved too quickly. "I'm going to remove the duct tape. Is that okay with you?"

Her fierce, but beautiful eyes softened if only a little, and she nodded, appearing resigned to her fate. Careful not to move too fast, he peeled the tape away from her mouth.

She drew in a breath and groaned at what had to hurt, although he'd been gentle with the tape.

Then her eyes sliced through him again and her mouth followed. "You're not going to hurt me? I was kidnapped, bound, gagged and stuffed in the lavatory of the plane you're on."

Ignoring her verbal attack for the moment, he reached behind her, cutting the plastic ties from her wrists with a knife from his ankle strap. Remaining guarded that she might try to harm him in some way, he cut the ankle ties, as well.

She rubbed her wrists and ankles, now free of the ties, clearly relieved to be rid of them. "Where are you taking me?"

While Connor watched her, he found two bottles of

water in the refrigerator. "Thirsty?" He held one of them out to her.

Giving him a wary look, she took the bottle and opened it. "It's not drugged, is it?"

Without waiting for his reply, she drank half the water. Her captors had left her for hours and now she was so thirsty she didn't care if the water was drugged? A burning sensation started in the pit of his stomach as his mind wrapped around the fact he'd found a kidnapped woman on the Learjet.

Connor sank into the seat across from her, uncertain how to reassure her.

"I told you already," he said gently. "I'm not the bad guy. I didn't kidnap you, and I don't know why you're on this jet. I'm just doing my job and flying it back to the rightful owner. But I'll admit, I didn't retrieve the plane on friendly terms."

What had he gotten into? He took a swig from his bottle. "So it appears someone stuffed you in the lavatory for safekeeping, intending to take you elsewhere and you're just my accidental passenger."

More like hazardous cargo.

THREE

Her honey eyes studied Connor's, looking for the truth in his words.

"Are you hurt?" he asked.

She looked down as though examining her body and seemed to notice her disheveled appearance. She shook her head, but he wasn't sure he believed her.

His heart ached. "Why don't you tell me what happened?"

Her well-defined dark brows furrowed slightly. "If you're not working with—" she stopped midsentence, hesitating, measuring her words "—my kidnapper, then who are you?"

Okay. He could give her that much. But he had the strong feeling she was about to tell him who had kidnapped her, and he had every intention of dragging that information out of her.

"The name's Connor Jacobson. I used to be a test pilot. And before that a fighter pilot in the Air Force." Maybe a little background would earn some of her trust. He drank more water while fixing his eyes on hers. "But now I'm…" He didn't finish. What exactly was he now?

"Maya," she said, and stared at the plastic bottle. She tugged a strand of her thick mane, the color of dark-roasted coffee, away from her face, revealing the shadows under her eyes.

"Maya?" he asked, hoping for a little more.

That's all she would give. It was enough for now.

Connor leaned forward, his elbows on his knees. "I have a feeling, Maya, that you might know more about what's going on than me. It would help me if you'd tell me what you know, like who kidnapped you for starters. And why."

"I haven't eaten since early yesterday." She avoided his eyes and rubbed her hand over the soft leather of the seat. "Do you have food to go with the water?"

Maybe, just maybe, she was beginning to believe him, though if he were in her skin, he'd be suspicious, too. He wished he knew how to completely convince her he wasn't involved in her abduction, but that was only one of the many problems her presence on the plane presented.

The woman had been traumatized, and Connor would give her the space she needed for as long as he could before he pressed her for information.

He glanced at his watch. She had half an hour. After that, he'd need time to make a plan before they landed.

Maya watched the sturdy pilot rise from his seat, never taking his eyes from her, as though he was suspicious of her. Finally he had to turn his back—hopefully, in search of food.

Why would he be suspicious of *her?* It's not as if she had a weapon or could hurt him. Though she had inflicted some damage to his jaw, *she* was the victim here.

How she wanted to trust him, to believe that God had sent someone to rescue her. But his story that he'd taken the plane and was flying it back to the rightful owner sounded so far-fetched it was difficult to believe. She knew the answer. She squeezed her eyes, reminding herself that her own situation was even more implausible. That's why she wanted to avoid telling him what she knew for as long as possible.

When she'd woken in the dark with a throbbing headache to discover her wrists and ankles bound, and duct tape over her mouth, she'd quickly determined she was in the lavatory of an airplane, though it was larger than most she'd been in on commercial airlines. The distinct sensation of takeoff confirmed it. She tried to stand and unlock the door, but with her hands bound behind her back, it was impossible to reach.

Her mind screamed with memories from the last time she'd been kidnapped and trapped in a small, dark room. The horrors and fear of that time, locked away inside all these years, had suddenly become reality again. And that reality went by the name of Roberto Hernandez. His face was the last thing she remembered seeing before everything went black. Among her vague memories of her abduction, she remembered hearing that Roberto had a Learjet waiting to cart her back to Colombia.

The man was head of the drug cartel that rivaled her father's, and he was the very same man who'd taken her as a child. Now he was back in her life. But why? Was he connected to her father's no-show?

Her well-meaning plans and hard work to change her life, to escape her heritage as a drug lord's daughter, hadn't made any difference. Even living in a country that seemed like a world away from her birthplace of Colombia hadn't kept her safe. She was back in the middle of hostilities between rivals, her limbs pulled and stretched by warring parties.

She had no idea how long she'd been out and given

that she ached all over, she had to wonder what they'd done to her. Who had drugged her?

The pilot? Was he in on this, though he claimed his innocence?

He returned with a plate filled with an assortment of pink and chocolate cupcakes decorated in multicolored sprinkles, and an apologetic grin at the corner of his mouth.

"I'm sorry I couldn't find anything more nutritious. The plate of sandwiches didn't make it on to the plane," he said.

"A sandwich would have been good," she said, taking a cupcake. "But thank you for this."

"At least a cupcake will tide you over until we reach Miami to refuel."

Miami? At least he wasn't headed to Colombia. For that she was grateful.

Ravenous hunger shoved aside her manners, and Maya ate one cupcake in two bites, licking the chocolate icing from her fingers.

She gazed up to find him still standing there, holding the platter. With his sun-bleached hair against tanned skin, strong jaw and cover-model looks, he was handsome as they came, but he also had a thoughtful gaze. Make that, concerned and distracted.

What was he up to in taking this Learjet? She got the feeling he was in the dark about the owner or else he wouldn't have lifted it. He had that wholesome, Eagle Scout air about him.

"Why don't you take the whole plate? You're hungry." He chuckled. "I'll get some napkins and more water."

She liked the sound of his laugh, and her earlier feelings of unease and suspicions were slowly fading.

A few seconds later, he sank into the seat across from

her again, holding the napkins and water. She ate slower now, and finished off her second cupcake, then took another bottle of water from him.

At some point, he was going to ask her again what she knew, and she'd play dumb as long as she could, but she had a few questions of her own. "So, you said you took the plane on unfriendly terms. What does that mean exactly, and who are you working for?"

He was sitting back now, his elbow on the armrest and his forefinger over his lips. He arched a brow at her questions. His hesitation told her he still had his own suspicions about her, and was considering his response. She didn't get that.

"Why don't you go first?" he asked.

Maya had been about to eat another cupcake but lost her appetite and put it back on the platter. "Isn't it obvious? I was kidnapped. I've got a lot more reason to be suspicious of you than you have to be suspicious of me."

"Maybe I can help you." Connor dropped his hand and squeezed the armrest. "Think. You have to know something. Who would want to kidnap you and why, for starters? For a ransom maybe? Or...did you get mixed up in something illegal? Maybe got in over your head?"

He had to be thinking she was selling drugs, of course, and someone had plans to make her pay. Or maybe he wasn't thinking along those lines at all. But to Maya, that was the obvious scenario. She looked away, hating that anyone could ever think that of her. But the truth was not much better, in her opinion.

If she could make it out of this and back home without ever having to reveal her father's identity and that she had planned to meet him, she just might make it home unscathed.

Please, God...

"I can see you're not ready to trust me yet. But let's at least be honest with each other. You know something. The name of your kidnapper was on your lips before you caught yourself. I have to wonder why you would keep that a secret."

"Someone kidnapped me—I'm the victim here. Why are you treating me like this? Why would you question me? Are you in law enforcement?"

Regret filled his eyes, and he placed his hand on hers.

"I'm sorry. I had no right," he said. "I'm trying to help you, that's all. I'll contact the authorities and explain what's happened, that we have a kidnapped woman on board."

He frowned, apparently not liking the sound of his words any more than she did.

"You can't do that," she said.

"Uh, Connor?" the other pilot called from the cockpit. "You'd better get up here."

"What is it?" he asked, but his Caribbean-blue eyes remained on her.

Of course, he wanted to know why she'd asked him not to contact the authorities. How could she explain?

"Connor. Now."

Maya shoved from her seat and followed him to the cockpit. The other pilot gave her a cursory glance, his full attention focused on the object soaring ahead of them outside the window.

"Why is there a fighter jet harassing us?" he asked. "Is there a reason the military would be after us?"

After dropping in the other chair, Connor assessed the situation. "That's not military—not anymore. It's an old out-of-commission fighter jet, an A-4 Skyhawk." The Skyhawk flew above and slightly ahead of them and rocked its wings. "Intercept aircraft. I don't see his wingman, but he wants us to follow."

Connor attempted to establish radio communication without success, which meant this intercept wasn't legitimate.

The other pilot huffed. "He's not responding? That figures, considering everything else that's gone *right* so far."

"In that case, he probably doesn't want to be identified." Connor rubbed his chin and looked behind him at Maya, his eyes boring into hers. "This just gets better and better. Uh, Jake, this is Maya, our accidental passenger. And this is my copilot brother, Jake."

Jake glanced over his shoulder at Maya. "Nice to meet you."

His eyes weren't convincing. "And you," Maya said.

"What do you make of it, then?" Jake asked, quickly turning his attention back to their dilemma.

"I think someone is either upset that we've taken their Learjet, or they're upset that we've taken their hostage, or both, and they're letting us know."

"And we're not going to follow them, right?" His brother's question begged for confirmation.

"Definitely not."

"Who is 'they,' anyway?" Jake cut a questioning glance to Maya, his eyes a similar blue to Connor's. "And how do we defend ourselves without weapons?"

When Connor didn't respond, his brother continued. "Come on, Connor. You're the fighter pilot slash test pilot. Got any tricks up your sleeve?"

Connor shook his head, his voice grave. "You know this plane isn't rated to make extreme maneuvers."

Maya felt an invisible hand squeeze her throat as if she could never escape Roberto, even thousands of feet in the air.

FOUR

"I'm calling for help," Jake said.

Connor squeezed the power lever, wishing he could take action. "Just who do you think is going to come to our rescue? And if we call for help now, they could shoot us out of the sky and be gone before anyone's the wiser."

"What are we going to do?" His brother ground out the words.

He didn't blame Jake. Connor never should have dragged his brother with him into this over-the-top recovery operation. Should never have agreed to get involved with this in the first place.

"What are we going to do?" Connor repeated the question, considering his options, which weren't many. Was he destined to go down again?

No. Thinking about his failures right now wouldn't do any good.

He looked behind him at the dark-haired beauty—the hazardous cargo he'd found on the Learjet who might end up costing them all their lives.

"You'd better take a seat and fasten your seat belt," he said.

"What...what are you going to do?" Maya hesitated in the doorway.

Connor cocked a brow. "You sure you want to find out the hard way?"

She disappeared into the cabin, and he gave her a few seconds before sending the jet in an arcing dive toward the earth.

"What are you trying to do, get us killed?" Jake asked. "You know we can't engage them."

"You just asked me if I had any tricks." Connor's palms slicked against the power levers, but his brother was right. Connor drew in a long breath. "Relax. I just wanted to see what the Skyhawk would do."

Connor leveled the Learjet, flying at thirty thousand feet. The Skyhawk stayed with them. If Connor didn't follow, would they be shot out of the sky? He wanted to outmaneuver the fighter jet, but he reined in the crazy thought. Like Jake said, that could get them all killed. He had more than himself to worry about this time.

This time.

His pulse rocketed as images bombarded him.

He was flying now, somewhere over the Mojave Desert when both engines died. The ground came at him fast, the experimental test plane dropping to the earth way too fast. There wasn't enough time. Seconds...he had seconds left, but they weren't enough. He ejected later than he should have, and then he slammed against the earth.

"Connor...Connor!" Jake's voice broke through the vision from his past.

Glancing at his brother, Connor drew in a breath. He'd spent months recuperating from his injuries after the crash, destroying the experimental plane he'd flown as a test pilot—another bird like this Learjet that cost in the millions.

Destroying his career and future.

Unlike the test plane, at least Connor had survived and all his body parts were in functioning order.

That was six months ago and it wasn't long enough to minimize his trauma. Still, it was enough to keep him from making an extreme attempt to outmaneuver the fighter pilot to his left. Regardless, he was in no position to engage in a dogfight.

"Give me a minute to think," he said.

"I'm not sure we've got a minute."

"In order to intercept us like this they had to have departed farther down our route and watched for us from anywhere in the Yucatán Peninsula, Haiti or Cuba. Then climbed to the same altitude and flown in a holding pattern, waiting for us," Connor said. "They had to know almost instantly that we'd taken this plane, and chosen this route."

"But we're too far into the Caribbean now and out of radar coverage," Jake said.

Connor glanced Jake's way. "GPS," he said, simultaneously with his brother.

"So they installed GPS tracking, probably because they were afraid someone was going to take their plane." Jake glared at Connor.

"As soon as we're out of this, find the GPS device so we can't be followed. Maybe it's somewhere in the cockpit and easy to dismantle."

"Who is this person, anyway?" Jake asked.

"Someone who wants this Learjet back," Connor said. "Thought we'd already established that."

"Just a guess, but seems to me we've picked a fight with someone who is powerful and dangerous." Jake glanced behind him, but Maya remained in the cabin. "What should we do now, turn around?"

What had Connor gotten himself, gotten them, into?

This was all too much and happening way too fast. "Are you kidding me? There's no way I plan to turn this plane around."

"Yes, I was kidding. But then again, what choice do we have?" Jake asked.

Connor couldn't stand the defeat he heard in his brother's voice. Incredulity raced through his veins, and he cut Jake a glance. "Like that's any choice? They'd kill us on the spot. They kidnapped a woman, remember?"

When Troy had hired Connor to recover this Learjet, he told Connor that a reputable businessman had fallen behind on his payments and all Connor needed to do was fly the jet back.

You might want to consider using the element of surprise...

Troy's words seemed to echo in the cockpit now. After everything that had happened, Connor understood the warning better, and he understood something else, as well—the man who had owned this Learjet was anything but reputable. Maya's presence just upped the stakes, but maybe they could come out of this like heroes.

The fighter jet flew closer then thrust ahead of the Lear, flying in front of them in a dangerous pattern. Connor wasn't impressed.

"Okay. I vote we call for help." Jake emphasized the last three words. "Someone needs to know what's going on."

Connor shook his head, cautioning him.

"Like I said before, you get on the radio now and they might decide to destroy all the evidence."

"They're not going to shoot us out of the sky," Maya said.

The sound of her smooth voice startled Connor. He hadn't realized Maya had left her seat and now stood behind him. She knew more than she was admitting, just as he suspected. "How can you be sure?"

"I can't. But I think the Learjet owner wants his plane back, and he won't get that if he shoots it out of the sky."

She didn't make mention that he wanted *her* back, as well.

"They're not going to follow us into U.S. airspace, either," Connor said.

"There's no need to. He already has people inside, and they'll be waiting for us."

The Skyhawk backed off and disappeared, and almost in unison, Connor and Jake released a long sigh. Connor looked over his shoulder. Maya had returned to the cabin.

"We need to change our passenger manifest before we land." Connor stood to leave the cockpit.

Jake eyed him. "You're full of bright ideas today. Just how do we do that midflight?"

"Figure it out and look for that GPS tracking device." He didn't have time for any of this. "I'm going to find out what Maya knows."

Just who exactly were they dealing with? He swiped a hand down his face as he paused before stepping into the cabin, hardly believing what had happened. How could he get answers from Maya?

Reg would know how to do it. Connor grimaced. Why did he have to think about Reg right now? His older brother's angry face filled his mind—the good son in the family with a successful career in the FBI. Connor didn't want to think about Reg's reaction should he find out what Connor had dragged Jake into.

He hadn't spoken to his brother in two years. *Always the failure, never the hero*—Reg's last words to him pounded against his already aching head. It didn't look as though Connor was anywhere close to changing that, despite his efforts today.

He shoved his failures aside. He needed to remain focused and keep a positive outlook, but this little mission wasn't looking nearly as advantageous as it had.

Maya searched the posh lavatory.

There...

Her pulse slowed a little. The men who'd taken her last night had crammed her bag into a small storage compartment. She still grappled with the fact that Roberto Hernandez had found her after over twenty years—and kidnapped her again. He'd gone to a lot of trouble to get her and because of that, she doubted she'd escape his claws this time. That fighter jet showed her just how determined he'd become.

But why now? What had happened to reignite his interest in her? She didn't doubt that her father had everything to do with it. She dumped the contents of her purse, which seemed considerably lighter, on the counter. Lipstick, a small brush, mirror and breath mints spilled out.

But no wallet.

Her heart skipped an awkward rhythm. That meant no cash. No credit cards. No driver's license. She dug inside the handwoven bamboo-and-satin bag. There. She felt something... Her hopes climbed.

Maya tugged out her passport. They'd taken her money but wanted her to be able to travel without raising questions. She stumbled from the lavatory, dropped into the rear seat, set her bag on the floor at her feet and pressed her passport against her chest.

Without this, she couldn't even make it back into the country. She drew in a few calming breaths. If she could just walk off the plane, slide through customs and evade

Roberto's men somehow, then she'd have a chance to consider her next step.

Without her passport, avoiding more trouble would be impossible.

Still, she was reduced to walking through this crisis moment by moment, one day at a time. Everything hinged on what the pilot intended to do with her. She'd been kidnapped and stowed away on his plane. Yes. But he wasn't involved with Roberto. That much she believed. Now to convince him to let her be.

She needed to handle this in her own way. She couldn't lose control of her life again. How could she make him understand?

Maya stared out the window at the Caribbean Sea passing beneath them. Soon it would change to the Gulf of Mexico as they traveled to Miami on what had to be a ninety-minute, maybe two-hour, flight.

She had an hour, if that, to figure things out. How much could she share with him and still hold on to what little of her life was left?

She only had herself to blame for the mess she was left with—she should never have agreed to meet her father.

One wrong decision and everything she'd worked for slipped from her grasp. How would she survive this? Even if she did survive, how would she escape and return unscathed, live the life she'd created without anyone being the wiser?

The pilot would want answers. She needed to tell him enough so he would understand how important it was to avoid contacting the authorities, and yet keep her identity and her life as secret as possible.

No one knew better than her, no one would understand that only she could solve this problem. Only she could connect with her father—for real this time—to discover why this man kidnapped her again. To discover what it would take to end this once and for all.

For twenty-plus years, she had deluded herself into believing she'd escaped Roberto for good. Roberto and her father were bitter rivals, and their feud could easily be taken right out of the headlines as they'd battled over territories for decades. He wanted to use her against her father, and the authorities would do the same if they discovered who she was. Her life would never be her own.

If the authorities knew her true identity, she'd be monitored, and then she could never safely make contact with her father again. Nor would she get the chance to say goodbye.

But Connor wouldn't understand, nor did she blame him. Maya pressed her hands over her face and rubbed her eyes. She heard the squish of leather and knew the pilot sat across from her.

Instead of acknowledging him, she coiled inside herself, wanting to stay hidden away as long as possible.

"You need to tell me everything." The deep timbre of his voice mingled frustration with betrayal, but she didn't hear the fear she expected. "Right. Now."

She dropped her hands and lifted her eyes to meet the piercing daggers in his. "Why do you look at me like that? I'm as much a victim here as you."

Her words didn't appear to move him with compassion. Not much, anyway. Still, she didn't miss the fleeting crease between his brows. Using a harsh tone with her pained him. He didn't like having to question her like this any more than she liked being interrogated. But she understood why he needed answers.

"You said, 'he already has people inside, and they'll be waiting for us.' What did you mean? Who are you talking about? We don't have time for games. Who kid-napped you?"

Why wasn't he terrified? Didn't he understand the danger they were in? Or was he a tough guy, a danger-ous man himself, for reasons she'd yet to learn? Maybe his Eagle Scout air was simply a facade. Who was he, really?

When Maya didn't answer, he leaned back in the seat as though he had all the time and patience in the world. Maybe he did. But he didn't know what she knew. "You don't have to tell me anything. You can tell the authori-ties when we land," he said.

Maya's heart jolted against her chest. He knew which buttons to push. Smart man.

"The man who kidnapped me, who owns this Learjet, is a powerful Colombian drug lord." She'd been pulled back into the Colombian drug wars, used as a pawn and stretched between the warring factions. Between Ro-berto and *her father,* but she'd leave *that* information out as long as she could.

"I see." Connor pressed his finger against his lower lip, contemplating her words. "Then why does he want you? What are you to him?"

This was the part where Maya needed to buy herself time, stall him as long as possible. Forever, if she could. And anyway she honestly didn't understand why she'd been kidnapped this time. She could only guess. "You should be more worried about the fact that you stole his Learjet. He will be waiting for you."

Roberto Hernandez had connections everywhere. That's why her mother had gone to great lengths to hide her over twenty years ago. Maya would have thought he'd forgotten her with so much time gone by. Now she doubted she'd ever find solace again until the man was dead.

The pilot shook his head. "We're landing in Miami. He can't get us there."

Maya prided herself on reading people and understanding their motivations. Despite her previous concern that he could be a dangerous man himself, Maya believed Connor considered himself a law-abiding citizen, and that what he'd done in taking the plane was aboveboard. He didn't understand that "right" and "wrong" didn't matter to Roberto. All he cared about was what he viewed as his property—and he'd go to any lengths to hold on to it…and punish those who took it.

"You don't know who you can trust, even there. Even if you remove me from the equation, you forget that you have just stolen a plane."

"I didn't steal the plane. I was acting as a recovery agent, representing my friend at a leasing company that owns it. For whatever reason, the payments—which are significant, by the way—have fallen into arrears. I have all the paperwork I need to recover the plane for the rightful owner."

"How much do you trust your friend at this company?"

The way the pilot's lips parted slightly, Maya knew she'd hit her mark. She'd created fear and doubt. And in doing so, she realized something herself. Roberto could have had all his assets frozen—including any front companies he might own in the U.S. Or maybe his cartel had been destroyed, making him more desperate than ever. That would explain why someone had sent Connor to repossess the Learjet he used, and why Roberto had gone to such lengths to kidnap her again before it was too late. He could torture her father and ransom her for the money he needed at the same time.

"Whether or not your repossession of this Learjet is

legitimate, our welcoming committee could ferry all of us back into Roberto's hands." The truth of her words snaked around her chest and squeezed.

Though he stared at her as if he believed she was crazy, she knew she'd planted the seed deep and that the pilot would give her words sufficient consideration. She needed him to focus on his own problems and allow her to take care of herself. That was her only hope for escape. Her only hope to return to the life she'd created—that is, once she found out how to end Roberto's pursuit of her forever.

"What are you suggesting?" he asked, a shred of alarm finally making an appearance in his blue-eyed gaze.

Maya opened her mouth to speak—

Connor's attention was torn from her by a muffled explosion.

FIVE

What's happening?

Connor looked out the window and saw nothing wrong. Nothing leaking from the right engine. No fire. No damage that he could see from where he stood, anyway. But he hadn't imagined the muted blast. Maya's reaction told him she'd heard it, too.

The Lear rolled to the right, throwing Connor into Maya. Time spilled into eternity as he found himself pressed against her soft, trembling body. When he searched her eyes—almost getting lost in their depths— he saw her terror.

Was she afraid they would crash?

Or more afraid they would land?

"I'm sorry." He gently extricated himself from her, his thoughts split between her and getting to the cockpit. "Did I hurt you?"

Her eyes locked with his, she shook her head. Suddenly, he wanted to make everything right for her. Protect her. He shook off the momentary insanity, ramping his mind back to reality. Everything crashed into him at once—retrieving the Learjet, Maya's kidnapping, the muted explosion outside the window.

The plane shook with a battering vibration.

Maya gripped the seat. "What's happening?"

"You'd better strap in." Connor left her and ran to the cockpit, a loud buzz resounding in his ears from somewhere in the back. He sank into the captain's seat next to Jake.

"Is it the engine?" Connor asked.

"That was my first thought, but the instrument panel, temperatures and oil pressures show normal."

Connor saw for himself that there was nothing different between the two engines. He took control of the plane, increasing speed.

"What are you doing?"

"Just trying something." Control response improved with speed, despite the shaking. "I guess I've flown enough experimental planes that my instincts sometimes take over."

The buzz morphed into a clacking sound—like a stick thrust into a big fan.

"How nice for you, but now we have a new sound, and no warning lights. What's up with that?"

Connor didn't miss the sweat beading on Jake's forehead.

"Just inform air traffic control that we need to make an emergency landing," he said.

"I don't think we're going to make Miami," Jake said, then contacted ATC.

"Lear 46RH, we understand that you are declaring an emergency due to a small explosion and violent shaking. Turn left to the Golden Key airstrip, descend and maintain 8,000."

Connor recalled what he knew of Golden Key. The resort island for tourists and the wealthy was just beyond the Dry Tortugas.

After Jake repeated the instructions, the air traffic

controller continued, "Lear 46RH please say souls and fuel on board."

Jake glanced at Connor. He knew Jake was thinking about Maya, their extra passenger. "Three souls on board and ninety minutes of fuel."

As Jake finished the conversation, Connor watched the instruments. The plane's vibration was starting to get to him. Maya had probably already crumpled in her seat by now. But there was nothing he could do to help her.

Then he saw it. "There it is. The right engine temperature is rising."

"The left is still good," Jake said.

"Let's shut the right down and run checklists."

"Whatever you say."

Connor smiled to himself in spite of the circumstances—Jake was a good pilot. He'd never flown with his brother, but the pressure was on, and Jake wasn't buckling under the crush. They shut down the right engine, and ran through the emergency engine-failure checklist to secure the failed engine.

"She's still shaking, still making the noise." Jake peered out the windows, as if he could see the answer out there, but only a mechanic could tell them what was wrong with the engine, and that, only after they'd landed safely.

"We're flying at altitude on the one engine," Connor offered. "We've done all we can do except pray."

"And land. We've done all we can do except land."

"We'll be fine, Jake."

"Don't tell me. You've flown under worse conditions." Jake's statement revealed his increased antagonism toward Connor.

"Okay, I won't tell you." Connor didn't think it was the time to share all his other concerns with Jake.

Jake excused himself to use the facilities, leaving Connor with his thoughts. And those thoughts turned straight to what Maya had said.

That she suggested he'd stolen this plane, committing a crime, burned his gut. No way would Troy send him to do something like that. Would he?

Still, the accusation made him a little nervous. In their risky escape, he wasn't even sure he had all the paperwork full of legal jargon. He'd stuffed it all in his jacket, he thought. He hadn't exactly used the documentation to climb on board and fly away as he'd expected. But he needed it on hand if asked. Connor didn't want to be digging through the paperwork when Jake got back from the bathroom. He'd wait until his brother had time to assimilate all that had happened.

Connor needed to buy himself enough time to work all the kinks out of this situation—to come out of it a hero this time. Funny that his attempt to gain some stability in his life, make his family proud of him, had landed him in this predicament in the first place.

So much for good intentions.

Connor squeezed the bridge of his nose and shut his eyes for a millisecond.

That was all the time he had to breathe.

In less than half an hour, the pit of venomous snakes he'd stirred up when he'd repossessed this Learjet might be within striking distance, if Maya's warning was true. She claimed that a drug lord had taken her, that Connor had taken his plane, and that he—or his men—could be waiting for them upon their arrival.

Was she for real? He wasn't sure he could trust her, but considering what they'd been through so far, it seemed safer not to doubt her, at least on that point.

And now…if they actually landed it wouldn't be

Miami as they'd planned. Not a big international port-of-entry airport where he could be sure he was dealing with the right people. Since it wasn't a port of entry, a Customs and Border Protection officer would have to meet them there. A small secluded island for tourists and the wealthy meant you could count on a few corrupt individuals, give or take.

In Connor's experience, he'd learned that customs at JFK might snarl at you, striking fear in your heart even though you committed no crime, but it always seemed to him as though customs at places where the wealthy landed private jets operated under a different set of rules.

Considering this drug lord's capabilities, things could be as Maya described. The man might have someone waiting there to retrieve his Learjet and abduct Maya again. Waiting there for Connor and Jake. But how could Connor know for sure? Regardless, he needed to prepare for the worst.

His brother returned to his seat and glowered.

"We have to talk about this," Jake said.

No kidding. "Look, I'm sorry—"

Jake cut him off. "But before we do, you need to visit with your girlfriend back there. She's not looking too good and didn't seem interested in giving me any information."

"My girlfriend? Hardly."

"Yeah, well, this whole thing was your idea. Now you've rescued a kidnapped woman—indirectly or accidentally, I'm not sure which, and I don't care. Helping her is a good thing, but I'm not sure how things will go down. From where I'm sitting, this all looks bad. Really bad."

Connor thought Jake had wanted to talk later, but apparently he couldn't hold his fury long enough. And Connor couldn't sink any lower—now he had Jake berating him. But his younger brother had a point. They didn't know what Maya would say when they landed. She could say *they* kidnapped her. At the moment, Connor needed to ensure that Jake gained control of his emotions.

"Panicking isn't going to help us."

"You're crazy, you know that? Why do I ever listen to you?" Jake drew in a long breath. "What's your plan now?"

"Take one thing at a time. First, did you find the GPS?"

Jake reached around his seat and held up a little box with a couple of wires hanging out. "With the way this day has gone, I'm surprised I didn't need to climb around outside the jet to dismantle it. We're fortunate it's one of the mobile kind."

Connor didn't want to voice his thoughts that their day wasn't over yet. "Good. At least we can't be followed. All we have to do now is make a safe landing. And as for everything else that's happened, this isn't anything we can't handle, but I think we might have bigger worries than how this looks." Connor shoved from his seat.

"Great."

"I'm going to see if I can find out more from Maya, and I'll let you know when I do."

"Don't take too long. We're about to start the landing sequence. I'm not sure how this thing is going to react."

Jake's words resonated through Connor—he wasn't sure what to expect from anything in his life anymore. This simple recovery of a Learjet had certainly not turned out as he'd expected.

The plane continued to shake as he made his way to Maya, ordering himself to get some real answers from her this time. Her honey eyes and dark mane were an intoxicating combination and sent his breath catching in his throat every time he looked at her. It made him way too easily distracted.

What was the matter with him? Okay, he'd admit that he was attracted to her, but that couldn't go anywhere. He couldn't let it. Not just because he wasn't sure he could trust her, but because he knew—from long, hard experience—that she couldn't count on him.

If his life had been different, maybe he would want a chance to be friends, maybe even something more. But as things were, he wasn't the kind of man women wanted for the long haul, and he would do good to remember that. He had the broken engagement to prove it.

Connor dropped into the seat across from her again, pulling her gaze and pensive thoughts from the window. The constant shaking unnerved her, and she feared they would end up in the azure depths of the Gulf of Mexico.

The handsome pilot's eyes swam with the blue-green of tropical waters, and though worry tugged at the corner of his lips, his soft smile reassured her. If she were a woman who believed in fairy tales, she could almost believe that he was destined to rescue her. That they were supposed to meet somehow, somewhere, but under different circumstances.

Why couldn't she have met him in the States, before she'd gone to Belize? Maybe he could have talked her out of going. But then again, once he learned the truth about her identity, he would have left her just as Eric had. Men could not be trusted.

Not her father. Not Eric. Not Connor. He would try to protect his own interests. She just had to convince him that those interests didn't include the truth about her, at least until she was free of him.

Turbulence jolted the fuselage, adding to her anxiety.

She squeezed the armrests, hating the vibration, the shaking, the turbulence—all of it—but holding on to her composure. She didn't want him to think her weak. She needed to remain strong in his eyes so she would have more negotiating power, should she need it.

"We haven't crashed yet. Does that mean we're going to live?" she asked, and even offered a smile. She needed to get on his good side, to convince him to listen to her plan.

He nodded. "Yes. I think chances are good we're going to live."

Maya wasn't sure if he would tell her otherwise. "To face another day," she added.

To possibly face Roberto's men when they landed. Of course, Roberto couldn't so easily take his plane back upon landing in Miami, but she'd wanted to incite fear in Connor. If he didn't know who he could trust, he wasn't as likely to tell anyone about the kidnapped woman he'd found on the plane he'd taken, and Maya's chances of walking away from this were much greater.

"To face another day." His smile grew wider, revealing two dimples on his left cheek.

She didn't trust his smile—he wanted her to let down her guard, using the same tactic she was using on him. She'd started it, after all, but sometimes a smile was all you had.

Though she tried to resist, she liked the curve of his lips. When she thought about it, she couldn't think of anyone she'd rather go through this with even though she knew little about him. But she knew enough—she sensed he was a champion inside.

Someone's champion, just not hers.

He didn't seem to realize that about himself, though, despite the confidence he projected.

"We'll be landing in a few minutes, an emergency landing at the Golden Key airstrip. It's small, but adequate."

His words wrapped around her throat and strangled her.

"Maya?" he asked. "Are you all right?"

"What happened to Miami?" She choked on her words.

"We're making an emergency landing because of engine trouble. What's wrong with Golden Key?" His soft, caring tone had turned brusque again.

"It's not far enough away, that's what's wrong."

She rubbed her temples. Maybe she was overreacting and should take heart in the way that she'd been rescued from Roberto's grasp. Maybe landing in U.S. territory would be her freedom. But no. Her instincts told her otherwise. Roberto's grasp reached into the Caribbean islands and the Keys—as had her father's, in years past. She doubted much had changed despite the government's best efforts. That much she could count on.

When she slid her hands away from her forehead, Connor studied her as if trying to determine if he could trust her.

She needed him to believe her, and the thought that he questioned whether or not he could trust her disappointed her on a far more personal level, surprising her.

"Do you really think this man has that kind of power that he will be waiting for us when we land?" he asked.

She drew in a calming breath. "Do you consider yourself a blessed man, Connor Jacobson?"

Contemplating a response, Connor stared at her, and when he didn't answer, she continued. "Once we land, if you have God's favor with you, then you might slip through his hands. But if you want to stay that way, if we are even given the chance, then we must go our separate ways."

A deep frown lined his face. Pain and compassion flickered across his gaze—the man was worried about her, more worried about her than himself. Her earlier misgivings about him—that he would try to protect his own interests at her expense—were wrong.

Such a small thing…Maya swallowed against the tightness in her throat…but that small thing had an enormous impact, touching a forgotten place in her heart that had long grown cold. The kindness in his eyes warmed her heart, overwhelming her, and giving her the sudden, crazy desire for him to wrap her in his arms, tell her it would be all right. She wished he would at least move into the seat next to hers—she needed to feel his nearness. Maybe she could draw strength from that.

But he remained in the seat across from her, watching her, the concern in his eyes disorienting her, confusing what needed to be a single-minded focus. Had it really been so long since anyone cared about her that a stranger could do this to her?

"I want to help you," he said.

What? No…

While she'd wanted him to be sympathetic to her plight as a victim rather than believing she was involved in the drug world, she didn't want to put him in any more danger.

Emotions warred on the inside while her father's drug wars battled on the outside.

Then there was the way this pilot affected her as if she was piloting an airplane over the Bermuda Triangle and into the electromagnetic vortex—her instrument panel spun out of control.

She glanced down at her hands still gripping the armrests, her nerves on edge enough without the plane's vibrating assault. Connor continued to watch her, waiting for her response—he wanted to help her, but he didn't know the full extent of the danger they were in. She couldn't allow him to get more entangled in her problems.

She shook her head, hating the burning at the backs of her eyes. No. She wouldn't cry. "You don't understand."

"Then explain it to me." Connor blew out an exasperated breath. "We've run out of time. Tell me what I need to know to do the right thing."

"Haven't I already told you enough? The man who wants me will not stop until he has me. Nothing and no one will stand in his way. You can't help me, so let me go away quietly. I need to disappear. Don't make any waves on my account. Don't tell anyone I was kidnapped. Leave the jet and the island. Get as far away as you can."

She hated watching the deep crease that appeared between his brows, but knew she'd hit her mark.

"Connor, some help up here, please!"

"We're not done with this discussion." His tone resonated with the pressure of the situation, the burdens he carried.

The pilot left her to assist his brother in landing Roberto Hernandez's Learjet that held Roberto's prize—the abducted daughter of his Colombian drug-lord enemy.

She squeezed her eyes shut and prayed, though she wasn't convinced a safe landing would do anything but offer her back into the hands of her abductor.

SIX

Hating that he had to leave his conversation with Maya unfinished, Connor slid into the seat next to Jake and stared at the instrument panel that indicated they were flying on one engine.

The clear blue sky staring back through the aircraft windshield belied their troubles.

They were only ten miles out now, and the airport was close, but with the shaking plane grating on his nerves, Connor wasn't sure it was close enough.

They'd have to land this bird in true emergency form. "I need you to run the emergency checklist for the engine shutdown in-flight again, and single-engine landing to make sure we didn't miss anything."

As the copilot, Jake worked through the tasks Connor, his captain, requested, including communicating with the tower while Connor focused on flying.

"With this shaking, I'm going to carry an extra ten knots or so until we get in close. Once our landing is assured, I'll call for the final flap setting. Let's stay sharp because a second go-around won't be an option."

Cleared for landing by the tower, Connor made the call for flaps eight, and Jake set the flaps at eight degrees, which increased the drag on the Learjet and aided in slowing it down.

The minutes ticked by as they drew near the airport. "Come on, come on, come on…" Jake said under his breath.

Did he realize he'd voiced his concerns out loud? Flying this piece of machinery on one engine wasn't that unusual, but the vibrating had both of them on edge. Maya, too.

"Flaps twenty," Connor called.

His copilot nodded and set flaps. Finally, Jake said, "Checklist complete, cleared to land."

"Gear down."

Next to him, Jake set things in motion. The hydraulic sounds of the landing gear lowering brought a measure of hope.

"Gear down and locked," Jake said.

"Landing is assured, full flaps."

"Full flaps selected…"

This time, the flaps significantly slowed the Learjet as Connor increased the descent rate onto the approaching runway. The jet met the runway and bounced once… twice…then stuck to the pavement.

"Thrust reverser," Jake called.

As the Learjet slowed on the runway, Connor released his pent-up breath.

"Okay, let's taxi to parking and shut her down." Connor swallowed to coax moisture into his dry throat. They'd landed safely but after everything Maya had said, he wasn't sure what to expect when they exited the Learjet.

As they cleared the runway, a couple of fire trucks approached. At a bigger airport, Connor could expect to see several emergency vehicles, but this was a smaller airstrip, only accommodating a few charter flights, private jets and commercial airliners during the busy season.

The jet parked and engines shut down, Jake sighed with relief.

Connor hadn't shared Maya's last words with his brother yet, though they'd hammered Connor's thoughts while he piloted the plane for a smoother-than-expected landing. He didn't need two pilots distracted until the plane was on the ground.

Still, the situation with Maya and the Learjet had to be forefront on Jake's mind, too, and he had to be anxious to hear what Connor had learned from Maya.

Granted, it wasn't much more than they already knew. Her words resounded through his mind.

"The man who wants me will not stop until he has me. Trust no one… Leave the plane and the island. Get as far away as you can."

He wanted to know more about this drug lord, but hadn't had a chance to ask before Jake had called him for assistance in landing the Learjet.

He spotted a man in a Customs and Border Protection uniform waiting until the all clear was given by the firemen. An invisible vise squeezed Connor's chest.

Trust no one…

"What did you find out?" Jake asked. "Did she tell you anything useful?"

"Not much, but enough. I don't think we're safe here. Don't say anything about anything. Understand?" Connor shot Jake his older-brother stare down, hoping that would be sufficient for now.

Jake returned his glare. "I want to know what she said."

"Just that we can't trust anyone on this island."

"And you believed her?"

"I don't know what or who to believe. I just know that we need time to figure things out. Can you give us that? Let me handle everything, okay?"

Jake scraped both hands down his face, then shoved his hair back. "Why did I ever agree to come with you in the first place? I could be lying on the beach in Hawaii right now, taking in the scenery."

Accepting that as Jake's agreement, Connor left his brother and exited the cockpit to find Maya wide-eyed, buckled and— Was she praying? Though she stared out the window, he could see her lips moving, reminding him of the many times he'd witnessed his mother doing the same, praying for her husband and her sons—praying for her family of pilots. Praying for her eldest, serving in the FBI.

But despite her prayers, his father had died anyway, doing what he loved. And despite Maya's prayers, they could face trouble anyway.

Connor still struggled to believe that Maya was on the plane he'd repossessed from, of all things, a drug lord. In a way, she was under Connor's protection, but if he wasn't careful, his compassion might grow into something more.

He could feel a soft spot forming in his heart where she was concerned, and watching her pray now considerably increased the size of it. The problem was he didn't want a soft spot. He didn't want to care about her like that—he'd been crushed before.

The other problem—she didn't want his help. He couldn't so easily shake his desire to protect her, but neither could he force the issue. Maybe that was for the best.

She'd been emphatic when she'd told him not to tell anyone she'd been kidnapped. To leave the plane and the island and her, getting as far away as he could. Connor struggled with what he should do.

"We need to exit the plane, Maya. We don't know what happened with the engine—it's not safe to stay here." The words slammed him—neither was it safe to leave the plane, according to what Maya told him.

At the sound of his voice, she startled. Rising from her seat, she gave him a look he couldn't read. What was it, fear? Dread? If only she could be relieved to be out of a foreign country and stepping onto U.S. soil. She could be landing in Colombia right now instead. She could be at the mercy of her abductor.

Or, she could be stepping right back into his hands. Connor prayed that wasn't the case. "I saw you holding your passport. You'll need that, I'm sure you know. The CBP officer is waiting for us."

"CBP?" she asked.

"Customs and Border Protection." If she'd traveled to Belize she should be familiar with that, but then again, maybe she hadn't thought of customs as CBP.

Nodding, Maya moved into the aisle, but said nothing. Connor grabbed the repossession papers he needed from his jacket, along with their general declaration forms stating the purpose of their trip. He'd stashed the jacket back in a bin. The Glock Jake had found at the beginning of their stressful flight went under a seat. He had no intention of declaring it, not wanting to make their situation more complicated when he faced customs. When he started toward the exit, she grabbed his arm. Connor peered back at her.

"Remember, keep your guard up. You don't know who to trust here. Roberto is looking for this plane. He's looking for me."

"Roberto? Roberto who? Why does he want you,

Maya?" Even as he asked the question, he knew he wouldn't get an answer yet. There wasn't any time.

"Roberto Hernandez." She opened her mouth to say more but terror infused her eyes before she looked away.

Connor frowned and turned his back on her to exit the plane. She followed him through the cabin.

Stepping from the jet, Connor was met by one of the firemen who gave him a thumbs-up. "You're good to go," he said.

Jake followed Maya down the steps. Together, they waited as the CBP officer walked around the plane with what amounted to a handheld Geiger counter.

Connor cringed—he'd completely forgotten about being fired upon. There could be dimples or even holes in the exterior of the fuselage, but then again, the guy wasn't making a detailed visual inspection. He was more focused on whether or not his device detected anything radioactive, and it would take a closer examination to see anything else. And anyway, Connor was only repossessing the plane—it wasn't his job to explain any neglect or disrepair.

Keep telling yourself that. He sent up a silent prayer.

The guy seemed official enough. Connor couldn't imagine him turning them over to the drug lord who was after Maya. Then again, he never imagined finding Maya on the plane, either.

He wanted to know more about this Roberto Hernandez and why he'd kidnapped her. Was she an innocent hostage or was she involved in the drug world in some way? Connor needed to guard himself where she was concerned, considering how much he already liked her and wanted to help her despite knowing next to nothing about her. When he looked in her eyes he found himself wanting to believe that she was simply a victim—but was that really wise? Or did she have the power to melt his better judgment when he was with her?

The CBP officer rounded the jet, snatching Connor's distracted thoughts back to the moment. Finished with his search for radioactive material, the officer turned his attention to Connor as the pilot. He handed over all the paperwork, including his documentation regarding his repossession of the plane. After what Connor thought was a casual inspection, the man requested their passports for examination.

Then he began his onslaught of questions. How long did you stay in Belize? Where else did you visit? How long were you there? The questions continued because the man was trained to be suspicious.

Something inside Connor's gut told him not to send out a flashing signal, to trust Maya's words. He prayed they could all act as though nothing out of the ordinary had happened. He didn't have to try hard—he wanted to believe her. Now, if only Jake would cooperate.

"Did anyone ask you to transport anything into the country?"

Connor almost choked on the question, considering the circumstances under which he'd transported Maya. If he was going to tell Customs and Border Protection about the kidnapped woman on the plane, now would be the time.

Though he didn't look at her for fear he'd give something away, he could feel the tension pouring from her. If he could, then the officer standing a few inches away probably could, too.

Or maybe it didn't matter—the CBP officer might be on Hernandez's payroll. When the official turned his attention back to Maya, Connor's doubts ramped.

The man smirked and returned their passports. "Enjoy your short stay in Golden Key."

Short stay? Was there a hidden meaning in his words? The hair on the back of Connor's arms stood at attention. He bristled, prepared for the worst, but the man turned and walked toward the small terminal that served the airstrip for the island.

"What now?" Jake asked. Hadn't he picked up on any of that? Or had Connor simply imagined it?

"We need to taxi the plane to the hangar for repairs," Connor said.

Jake climbed back into the Learjet.

Maya turned to face Connor then, her dark, Hispanic complexion ashen. "Thank you for what you did," she said.

"Who was that man, Maya? Why did he look at you like that?"

"The less you know, the better. We should go our separate ways now. You should leave the plane and the island like I've already told you."

"Delivering the plane comes with a hefty paycheck, one that I can't give up without good reason."

"Is it worth your life? Or that of your wife?"

His wife? "I'm not married. Not even engaged—anymore."

Was this guy that much of a threat? All the more reason for Connor to question Maya further.

"What does he want with you? I'm more concerned about your life right now." Connor stared at the clear blue sky, which contradicted the ominous situation. "We're going to taxi the Lear into the hangar so a mechanic can look at it. You can come along for the ride and tell me everything."

Maya shook her head and turned her back on him,

leaving him to watch her walk toward the terminal in the distance, the same building where the CBP officer had gone.

"Maya, wait…"

"Connor, you coming or what?" Jake asked.

What was it with his brother and his timing?

Leaving her to fend for herself felt wrong. All wrong. But he couldn't make her accept his assistance.

So much had happened in a short period of time, Connor wasn't sure what to think. He didn't want to have a knee-jerk reaction to any of it. There was no doubt that she'd been kidnapped and someone had meant her harm. No doubt they'd been shot at as they taxied down the airstrip in Belize, and no doubt they had been warned by an old fighter jet. Could any of those threats actually follow them onto U.S. soil? Onto this island?

Connor tugged his gaze from her, ignoring the burning in his gut, and climbed back into the jet. How could he help her if she wouldn't let him?

Maya's pulse hammered in her ears as she took one step, then another, away from Connor and toward the small terminal. She wasn't even sure she could call it an actual airport, though she spotted a few jets and bigger planes.

Still, they'd made it. They'd landed and now they were back in the U.S. She pressed toward the building, feeling the pilot's gaze on her back. Funny how a person could sense when someone watched them.

One step. Then another.

Though her heart still raced, she wished she could breathe easier now—this wasn't Colombia. Things could have turned out so much worse. Connor's repossessing the Learjet had saved her from her fate. For now. Connor likely didn't believe her about the danger they were in because of their uneventful arrival. But she couldn't worry about that. He could take care of himself. She'd warned him. That was all she could do for him and his brother.

At least he hadn't mentioned the kidnapping to the CBP officer—but she wasn't sure that mattered in view of the look the official had given her. She'd shuddered beneath the smirk that had made her suspicious of the man. Was he working for Roberto? Would he report her location now? Is that what he meant regarding her *short* stay?

Goose bumps spread over her arms—she sensed she wasn't out of danger yet.

Why, oh, why had she left Connor's side? His protection? She'd felt much safer when she was with him, the keen sense of his absence washing over her as if she'd fallen into an ice-cold, rushing river. He'd offered to help, but what could he do when he didn't understand what he was dealing with?

What could he do if he did?

At the corner of the building, she spotted a pay phone. With no money, at least she could make a collect call to her mother and let her know what had happened, then make a plan to leave the island.

Still niggling at the back of her mind was the fact that she would never be safe again until Roberto was dealt with. Maya would need to contact her father, too, and hope he could do something about Roberto.

"God, protect me," she whispered under her breath. "Give me justice." But would justice cost her her own life before Roberto was held accountable for his crimes?

Stepping up to the pay phone, Maya touched the handset and froze. Her skin tingled.

Someone was watching her.

SEVEN

Tension knotting his shoulders, Connor stepped from the shadows of the hangar where he and Jake had left the jet with a mechanic. The midafternoon sun forced him to squint until he tugged his shades from his shirt pocket and put them on.

The mechanic didn't know the reason for the vibration or the noise, but had said he would call Connor as soon as he figured it out. Did the trouble have anything to do with the bullets that had pelted the plane when they'd left? Had one lodged in the wrong place? He glanced at the two private jets parked near this hangar.

Given the kind of people who frequented the island, there was a good chance the jet could be repaired here, but he didn't know how long it would take. Could Connor trust the mechanic to be honest on that point? Or would he purposefully keep him waiting so that Hernandez could retrieve his plane?

All the more reason Connor needed to get in touch with Troy. Find out what he knew about Roberto Hernandez—the man he'd sent Connor to recover the Learjet from. Plus, someone needed to pay for the repairs. But right now, Connor wasn't sure he could even trust Troy, considering he hadn't been completely forewarned about the clientele before he'd retrieved the Learjet.

Maya had driven suspicion into his every thought with her words.

Just leave the plane.

Leave the island.

Trust no one. He wished he could do what Maya had said.

But getting the plane back to Troy would mean a substantial amount of money and it would be his paycheck to buy his business, to get a new life—that is, if he could trust the man.

When Troy had contacted him and offered this opportunity to earn his wings back, so to speak, his first niggling question had been, why Connor? Why not someone who had experience recovering a plane in arrears?

Maybe because Connor was desperate enough for this particular job? It was a risky business, after all. But he was accustomed to that, wasn't he? Being a pilot usually made the top three of the most-dangerous-jobs list as it was.

Or maybe because when Connor had served in the Air Force as a fighter pilot, he'd ejected from a crashing F-22 Raptor and had survived in the Iraqi desert.

Maybe because of his reputation as a daredevil test pilot? Or because he was certified to fly more than his fair share of aircraft.

Any of those reasons could mean he was the man for this particular hazardous job.

But none of them mattered now. He was here.

One last risky job.

Standing there in the sunlight, surviving the crazy bullet-laced takeoff in one country and landing with one engine in another, Connor wanted to feel as though he'd successfully cleared a few obstacles—but the knot in his gut told him he'd only just entered the obstacle course.

Where was Maya?

He glanced around, searching for her. Knowing he shouldn't have let her walk away.

Idiot—he was an idiot.

His next breath caught in his throat when he saw her—she stood a few hundred yards away at a phone booth at the side of the terminal. He watched her wary, searching glances around the airstrip as if she expected someone to land and take her away any minute. She must have made multiple attempts to reach someone if she was still there.

Next to him, Jake released a weighty sigh. "Well, what next?"

"I'd say you don't have to wait for the repairs, except I still need to fly the thing out of here," Connor said.

"I thought you didn't think we were safe on this island based on whatever Maya told you? Change your mind already?"

"No. I haven't changed my mind." He watched Maya, aware that Jake stared at him, waiting for an explanation. "You fly to the Keys all the time, right? Ever spent any time here?"

Jake nodded and narrowed his eyes.

"Know a good place to stay?"

"I know a place where we could crash for a few hours, maybe even days, if you're considering staying." Jake squinted in the bright sunlight. "But Maya's trouble, Connor. Don't tell me you're thinking of bringing her with us. Why'd she say we aren't safe here? Why do you believe her?"

"Let's crash somewhere while we find out more about what's going on. None of us is thinking clearly right now. It's hard to imagine her kidnapper could find her now or find his plane, but I didn't like the vibes coming off the CBP officer."

"I think you're being paranoid. But whatever."

Connor glanced behind him and into the shadows of the hangar, spotting the CBP officer talking to the mechanic. An eerie chill ran over him. "We need to leave now." And find some place to hide.

"I'll make a call."

"An old girlfriend?" Connor would find out soon enough but was curious to know.

"Just a friend." Jake glared at Connor. "Really. She lives with her mother."

Jake cleared his throat and tugged out his cell, turning his back to Connor.

With that, he left Jake to make arrangements for them and marched to the terminal where Maya stood near the southeast corner, still making a phone call on a pay phone.

When she saw him, she hung up and looked away.

"Have you found a ride out of here yet?" he asked. He'd seen her passport, but did she have any cash or credit cards in that bag she carried? He hadn't exactly had time to grill her on those details.

Though her brows creased and her lips grew tight, she continued to avoid his eyes.

"No?" he asked, tossing her a wry grin.

Maya's gaze jumped to his. She didn't return his smile. Instead he saw fear in her eyes, and he didn't miss the state of total fatigue on her face and in her posture.

"Jake has friends on the island that we can stay with until we figure things out. Wait on the jet to get repaired, and when it is maybe we can even fly you home, wherever that is. In the meantime, you can make all the phone calls you want on my cell."

"I don't know what to say." Her honey eyes searched his, but remained serious and—could it be?—hopeful.

Her reply lifted a weight from his shoulders he hadn't known he carried. That she was actually considering accepting his help and invitation surprised him, especially after her instructions to leave the island. Still, her spirits hadn't lightened one bit, even now that they'd landed safely and she was free from her captors, but Connor knew why—she didn't believe she'd escaped yet.

Neither did Connor. That's why it was more important than ever to convince her to stay with him.

"Say yes. You have to be tired and hungry. I know I am." Connor smiled, wishing he could shove aside that nagging sense that they were still in danger. Just for the moment, he needed to reassure Maya.

Before he told another soul about Maya or what had happened, Connor wanted to know more just in case she was right about a drug lord owning people on the island, putting them at serious risk.

On a hunch, a crazy hunch at that, Connor held out his hand. His throat grew thick as he waited. He wasn't sure why he'd offered his hand. But would she take it?

The hint of a smile formed in her right cheek. Connor realized he'd only seen a small, wary smile from her since he met her—with good reason—but he wanted something with high-wattage shining from her lips. Why she affected him so personally, he wasn't sure. She hesitated, then finally lifted her hand and slowly placed it in his.

Her palm was warm, soft and small, making Connor feel as if he was holding a delicate and rare bird—but he knew better. She was anything but delicate. In that moment, with her hand in his, he knew he needed to see this through with her, if she'd let him. But it could be dangerous to his life and...to his heart.

Though Jake would have to decide for himself whether to see this through, Connor hadn't spent his life taking risks just to stop now. Their lives had been thrown together in survival mode. He could only hope the worst of it was over, but something told him it wasn't.

Admittedly, Maya was glad to see Connor. Standing next to her, his shadow covered her completely, protecting her from the sun and hiding her from danger, whether imagined or real.

With his lean, athletic physique, she wished that he could protect her. Relief rushed through her like warm water filling all the cold, empty places, and calming her panic-stricken heart.

Would he believe her if she told him she sensed someone was watching her? Or had it been Connor watching her from a distance that had given her that feeling? No. She felt something entirely different when she'd known he was watching.

Warmth.

Maya's relief was palpable and she released a sigh. Without her wallet, she couldn't even get a cab to leave the airport. She was desperate. Under Connor's gentle, reassuring gaze, Maya's decision that she shouldn't involve him in her predicament wavered.

When she first realized he'd saved her from Roberto's men and a flight to Colombia, she'd thought God had sent him. Maybe she shouldn't walk away from him just yet.

Though she needed to get off this island, she wasn't sure where she would go. Home didn't seem like a wise move at the moment. She'd already made the biggest mistake of her life as it was, and couldn't afford another one. The call or two she'd planned to make had been a waste of time—she couldn't get through.

Still holding Connor's hand, she savored the strength in his grip and didn't want to relinquish her hold. Though wary of everyone and everything around her at the moment, she wanted more than anything to believe what his eyes told her now—what they'd told her before on the plane. He cared. He wanted to help. But why?

Were there really any good people left in the world? Maya cringed at her negative thoughts. Exhaustion was taking a toll.

No longer able to meet his intense blue gaze, she averted hers. She owed it to him to warn him again, give him another chance to walk away, despite her faltering resolve. "You shouldn't get involved with me."

"Looks like I'm already involved, don't you think?" He eased his hand away, leaving hers cold and empty, missing his sturdy grip and reassurance.

Maybe she needed someone strong on her side. Someone to help her get control of her life back. Someone else who knew the full truth of her predicament. But Maya struggled to answer. She didn't want to drag him even deeper—he didn't have a clue, but he was right. To think this through clearly she needed rest and food.

It could mean the difference between life and death.

She inhaled, drawing in the strong odor of jet fuel and the aroma of island food—someone must be grilling nearby. "Okay. But just until I can make other arrangements."

His smile had amazing power over her distraught state of mind, and her spirits lifted a little, giving her what had to be false hope that she would live at least another day without seeing her father's nemesis.

EIGHT

Connor's brother secured a cab that would take them to a friend's house.

Maya had never been to Golden Key, or any of the Keys for that matter, and as the cabbie drove, she gazed out the window, taking in the strange mix of mobile homes and gated, upscale communities. The trauma of the past several hours had jarred loose memories from her short life in Colombia. Visions from her past that she didn't know she possessed accosted her now, overlaid on the streets of Golden Key. Evil men toted machine guns, shooting in rapid-fire succession. People screamed and fell. Blood oozed. Maya shuddered, fearing she would see that same scene on the streets before her now. And there was no one—neighbors, policemen or the military—that could be trusted.

She shut her eyes. A warm, strong hand grabbed hers and squeezed, sending the visions from her past running.

"It's going to be all right," Connor whispered, his gentle tone wrapping around her.

She wanted to believe his words, but he didn't know what he'd gotten into. Still, she opened her eyes to take in as much of the island as she could, and watch for anyone suspicious.

Charming, almost dilapidated restaurants remained standing next to newer, more chic places to accommodate the wealthy residents and tourists. People—visitors and locals alike—strolled streets, giving the place an odd air of the casual and laid-back mixed with the feel of a Club Med resort.

The cabbie drove past a flea market hugging the coast and then turned down a curb-less street lined with thick trees and palms shading the houses. He pulled into the driveway of a small, pink stucco bungalow. Maya wondered if this was a rental home for vacationers, or if Jake's friends were locals who lived here year-round.

Behind her temples, she felt the pounding she'd woken up with in the Learjet lavatory return. All she wanted was a long hot bath, a good meal, a soft bed and then freedom from Roberto, bringing closure to a long chapter in her life. But she needed answers before she could ever get her hands on the latter.

Connor paid the cab driver, then climbed out and assisted Maya. She stepped onto the lawn and weaved her fingers through her hair, pulling it out of her face. Jake walked ahead of them to the front door of the house. The door opened and out stepped a tall, big-boned brunette along with another woman who was simply an older version of the first—her mother? Sister? Jake was greeted warmly and he turned and smiled at his brother, gesturing for Connor and Maya to follow.

Jake introduced Cheryl and her mother, Karen.

"It's nice to meet you, Maya," Cheryl said.

Maya didn't miss the slight hesitation in Cheryl's smile as she took in Maya's appearance. Though Maya didn't want to draw more attention to herself, she couldn't help but glance down at her attire and realize how haggard she looked. Her crumpled shirt and slacks boasted a tear or two—telling her she must have fought with her abductors at some point, despite the drugs. Maybe she'd awakened and they'd had to drug her again.

But she couldn't remember a thing, and that realization terrified her like a dark thunderhead threatening to move in and destroy the small hope she now harbored.

Maya forced a smile. "Thanks for opening your home to us on such short notice."

She glanced at Jake, hoping that she hadn't gotten her information wrong, but the pleasantries continued as they were escorted inside. Guilt engulfed her—Cheryl and her mother could be more people dragged into this dangerous drama.

Trembling began in her knees and worked up her legs. After everything she'd been through, she needed a good, long cry, but Maya hadn't given herself the luxury of tears since she was five. She had to continue to be strong to make it through this.

While Jake talked to Cheryl and her mother in the kitchen decorated in bright colors, Connor stood in the middle of the warmly paneled, cozy living room. Hands plastered on his hips, he stared out the two large windows at the front of the cottage as though analyzing how much protection this place could offer them, if any.

Though he'd told her everything would be all right and had reassured her by his mere presence, his watchful gaze also told her he hadn't let down his guard. It seemed as though he was still wary and believed Maya's pursuers were possibly out there somewhere on this island. *His* pursuers, as well—because he'd taken the Learjet and their captive on board—were out there, and had learned of Connor, Jake and Maya's arrival.

She'd thought Connor was someone's champion,

though he didn't realize that about himself. Maybe he really was her champion.

The thought of it brought a smile to her lips despite the precarious circumstances. She hoped she'd get the chance to thank him properly, though she wasn't sure how. Maybe somehow she'd find the chance to make him understand how much his help meant to her.

Before she could look away, he'd caught her staring. He returned her smile. "That's beautiful, by the way."

Confused, she gave a subtle shake of her head. "What?"

"Your smile. That's the first time I've seen a real one from you, which is…understandable. What were you thinking just then?"

That you're a champion, maybe my champion…but she couldn't bring herself to say the words.

"I…uh…" Maya considered her thoughts leading to the smile. One second she wanted to cry and the very next she'd smiled? She was losing it for real now. She covered her face with her hands.

"Maya," Cheryl whispered and gently squeezed her arm. "Let me show you to your room. It's connected to a bathroom where you can freshen up."

Dropping her hand, Maya managed another smile for these hospitable people. For Connor and his brother. Connor didn't return it this time, and shared a look with his brother instead. A deep frown creased Jake's forehead. Between the two of them, Jake was the one she feared trusting with her secret. But once she told Connor, and she'd have to eventually, Jake would learn the truth, too. Connor wasn't likely to keep that kind of information from his brother. How could she expect him to?

Cheryl led Maya down a long hallway and into a small bedroom in muted shades with a light gray tiled floor. The room had Pottery Barn furniture and a blue checkered quilt covered the bed. A Van Gogh print hung over it. The room was warm and inviting. Maya eyed the soft mattress and all she wanted to do was fall down on it and sleep for a hundred years. Cheryl must have read her thoughts because she crossed the room and closed the shades, shutting out the sunlight.

"I don't think I have any clothes that would fit you, but Mom might. You look like you could use a long, hot bath." She smiled. "Am I right?"

"I would love one, thank you."

Cheryl opened a door connecting a bathroom. "Everything you need—towels, shampoo, bubble bath and body wash—is in there. While you take a bath, I'll find you something clean to wear, and I'll lay the clothes out on the bed for you. Will that work?"

Out of nowhere, Maya's words to Connor dropped into her mind. *Trust no one.* Maya's breath caught in her throat. Was she making a mistake trusting Cheryl? *Please, God, no.* She wanted to trust this woman. She needed rest or she couldn't think straight. But what had Jake told Cheryl?

Was Maya a fool to trust anyone? The room swayed and Cheryl's smile morphed into a frown as she steadied Maya. "Are you going to be okay? Should I call a doctor? Or—"

"No," Maya replied a little too emphatically. "No, I'm fine. All I need is a bath and a nap," she said. "Thanks."

Though Cheryl didn't look convinced, she nodded. "Okay, as long as you promise to let me know if there's anything else I can do."

Maya could hardly look Cheryl in the eyes and ran her hand over the quilt. "I promise," she said.

After Cheryl left, Maya took the long, hot bath she'd

been dreaming of ever since Connor mentioned finding a place to rest. The scorching hot bubble bath foamed around her and she closed her eyes, allowing the water to wash away the grime and—if it were possible—the memories of the past few hours. She wasn't sure she could even afford the time to do this, but this could be her last reprieve for a while.

Much too soon the water cooled off and Maya left the small comfort of the bath. Afterward, she found some baggy sweats and a large T-shirt on the bed. Cheryl had left her some clothes as promised, but they didn't fit very well. Still, if this was all the woman had to share with her, it was enough. She put them on and climbed under the sheets, giving herself permission to rest for an hour.

Then…then she would make the call to her mother. And then she would call her father. He would know why Roberto was after her. He would know what to do.

And if not, then Maya wasn't sure she would survive this time. But for now she shoved thoughts of Roberto away and thought about Connor.

She reminded herself that men couldn't be trusted. Her father had let her down because of the path he'd chosen. Eric had let her down when he'd learned about her father.

And Connor would let her down, too, eventually. He couldn't be her champion. Despite the reminder, his handsome face, his warm, Caribbean-blue eyes, filled her heart and mind.

NINE

While Jake sat in the kitchen and talked to Cheryl and her mother, Karen, Connor peeked through the curtains he'd discreetly drawn over the windows, shutting out the view of the yard, trees, palms and the street. Neighboring houses could be seen through the trees along with the beach a short distance away.

No doubt Cheryl had noticed he'd taken the liberty of closing her curtains, but she said nothing. Maybe she thought Connor planned to take a nap in the recliner and wanted the room dark. If Hernandez knew where they'd landed and was searching for them, he wouldn't know to look here—that would at least buy them some time.

And Connor needed time to figure out this whole mess. For starters, he needed more information about Hernandez, the drug lord who wanted his Learjet back and Maya along with it. Connor wanted to know who she was to the drug lord and why he'd kidnapped her.

When Maya was near him, he couldn't think clearly. In order to get her to safety—and he had every intention of doing just that—he needed to ignore how she affected him. But how?

Connor reminded himself that she could have fooled him all along. Maybe she was a drug dealer herself and that's why Hernandez was after her. As hard as he tried, he couldn't believe that about her. It seemed that turning a cold heart to her was already a lost cause.

Still, he needed the whole truth from her. Though she needed some respite—they all did, after what they'd just been through, he couldn't wait forever.

In the meantime, Connor needed to have words with Troy at Genesis. He clenched the phone in his hand, furious with how he'd been tricked into believing this job was just a simple task—recovering a jet from a once-wealthy businessman going through tough times.

Right.

Did Troy know the man was a drug lord? Did he know the drug lord had kidnapped a woman? Was Troy in on it? For all Connor knew, Troy couldn't be trusted.

Nah. He'd known Troy for years. Any misgivings about that part of the situation wouldn't stick. Troy was clueless, too. That had to be it. Connor couldn't stand to think otherwise. All the blame laid with Troy's client—the Learjet owner, or rather lessee, who was just a number to Troy.

When he made the call to Troy, letting him know the jet would need repairs, Connor would leave out the part about the kidnapped woman to see if Troy said anything suspicious.

He frowned—Maya had become more than a kidnapped woman to him, he'd already decided. How quickly she'd burrowed into his heart. Was it because of his deep need to save someone? Be a hero? She was desperately in need of saving, he'd give her that. If only he could shove aside the baggage he'd carried into this situation. His issues were definitely clouding his judgment.

Before he dialed the number his phone rang. The Golden Key Airport.

Connor answered.

"This is Steve at the hangar. I found the problem. Something caused the shaft bearing to fail and dislodge the shaft. The blades got chewed to pieces and pulverized the shaft. That's why the plane vibrated."

That would account for the noise, too. Connor instantly thought of the bullets that hit the plane when they took off from Belize—the mechanic had apparently been too focused on the engine trouble to give the fuselage a closer look because he hadn't said anything about dings or holes. Connor hadn't had a chance to inspect the plane himself and he didn't want to draw any unwanted attention. Nor was he about to ask the man if he'd found a bullet, or if a bullet could have caused a turbine shaft bearing to fail and dislodge the shaft. "And?"

"It'll take me a week and a half if I rush it."

"What'll it cost?" Connor squeezed the bridge of his nose, knowing it wouldn't be cheap. After the mechanic gave him all the details, Connor made the call to Troy and explained the situation.

"What? I need that plane flown to the mechanic in Richmond, not hundreds of miles away."

"Really? You expect me to fly that far on one engine? In a shaking plane?" Connor leaned his head against the wall and watched out the window, letting Troy vent his frustration. A topless Jeep full of kids enjoying the afternoon sun sped by, driving too fast through the neighborhood.

Wishing he could trade places with them, he pictured Maya by his side and that took him by surprise.

"Connor...Connor, you still there?"

"Yes. Are you done berating me? Because I have a few words of my own."

"I'm listening."

"I get why you said I should use the element of surprise, but I wasn't expecting to face off with men holding submachine guns. I wasn't expecting to be shot at while I taxied down the runway."

And I wasn't expecting to find a kidnapped woman on board. Troy hadn't said anything suspicious, convincing Connor that the man wasn't in on the abduction. Still, he resisted the urge to tell Troy about Maya. Something inside told Connor to keep Maya's presence a secret, to keep her hidden. She was under his protection.

Silence met him on the line at first, then, "Maybe you should have expected that. People don't like to let go of their luxuries."

"You could have said more, that's all."

"Would you have taken the job if I had?"

"Oh, I get it. You couldn't find anyone else for this one, so you thought I'd be more than happy given that I was down on life. Way to kick a friend when he's down, Troy."

Troy sighed. "I'm sorry, Connor. I really didn't know it would be that bad."

Connor heard the regret in Troy's voice, but he wasn't done with his own venting yet. "This could have ended a lot worse than just you having to wait on your plane."

"Look, I honestly didn't know someone would shoot at you, okay?"

Didn't he? "Who is this guy, anyway? Because I'm not buying he's just a rich man who likes to travel and has suddenly gone bankrupt." *Do you know he's a powerful Colombian drug lord?* But telling Troy that much might give away the rest, and he wanted to find out what Troy knew.

"Look, Connor. These things can get too complicated to go into the details. In the end, it all boils down to what I told you. I'll send you part of your payment now, that way you can have some fun while you wait. It's the least I can do."

More money wouldn't help him in his current predicament with Maya. "You can count on me to fly it the rest of the way when it's ready, but I have a feeling this guy isn't going to let go so easily. He might try to take his plane back."

Troy chuckled. He didn't believe Connor? "This job isn't for the faint of heart, that's why I thought it would be perfect for you. But if I need to get someone else to fly it home…"

"Like I said, you can count on me. Nothing has changed."

"That's good to know."

"One more thing."

After giving Troy the mechanic's number so he could make payment arrangements, Connor ended the call, feeling only mildly placated.

"Everything okay?" Jake entered the living room, a look of expectation on his face.

"No. How's that for an answer to your loaded question?" Connor tossed Jake a wry grin. "Everything good with you and your girlfriend?"

"I told you we're just friends."

"I'm not sure she agrees, considering the way she looks at you."

"If I was going to take advantage of her, I would have already done it." Jake glared. "I've changed."

"You've changed? And what brought this about?" Connor wanted to believe his younger brother.

The distant, regretful look in Jake's eyes startled Connor. "Don't tell me. Someone actually broke *your* heart?"

Jake's pointed stare was answer enough.

Connor wanted to know more, but this wasn't the

time to dredge up anyone's past. They had bigger problems. Connor blew out a breath. "I'm sorry. I shouldn't have said it like that."

Silenced passed between them for a few seconds, then Connor finally broke it. "I'm just grateful Cheryl and Karen gave us a place to crash."

"That's great that you're appreciative." Jake poured on the sarcasm. He strolled by and plopped on the sofa, clasping his hands behind his head. "So what are we going to do about *your* girlfriend?"

Connor ignored Jake's attempt to bait him as he peeked through the curtains again. Nothing. He shoved aside his constant concern that someone would find them, and thought about Maya. Again.

They weren't even friends—he needed the reminder. He hardly knew Maya and certainly didn't know her secrets. And yet he'd already proclaimed himself her protector and had said he would see this through to the end. He couldn't envision it any other way.

"I sense you're trying to figure out how you can save a damsel in distress."

Connor hated that Jake had come close to hitting the mark. Hated the truth in his brother's words. This couldn't be about Connor saving his reputation. He wouldn't let it be about that. But God had put Maya in his path. He knew that, and he wouldn't let her down. Wouldn't let Troy down, if he could help it.

He would prove Reg wrong this time. "I need to protect her and in order to do that, I need to find out who is after her."

"You mean protect the Learjet. Find out who is trying to recover the Learjet."

"That, too."

"I'm glad you feel that way. Now we've come to that moment in time where you need to tell me everything."

"That's going to be a problem. I don't know everything yet."

Why hadn't Maya been willing to open up? He hoped that now she trusted him enough to tell him. Their lives could depend on it.

Her father called her name from the end of a long hallway. He disappeared behind a door. Maya ran after him but the corridor only grew longer for her efforts. She ran harder. Faster. Her legs grew tired and her breathing labored. The door he'd gone through was farther away now, instead of closer.

Get. To. The. Door.

You'll be safe there, *a familiar voice told her. But she couldn't remember whose voice.*

Roberto Hernandez laughed from behind. Somehow she knew he was closer now. He wanted to kill her.

Maya sat up, coming fully awake and gasping for air after a terrible dream. Where was she? She glanced around the small airy room and everything rushed back.

How long had she been asleep? She'd climbed into bed around four-thirty. She grabbed the clock from the nightstand and focused, still struggling to breathe.

Eight-thirty? She'd only intended to rest for an hour—it was later than she'd planned. She couldn't stay here… though she didn't know where she'd go. To think, only a few days ago her life was normal except for the lie she'd lived, hiding her past. All these years, she'd lied to herself.

Maya threw her legs over the side of the bed and noticed a glass of orange juice and a plate of bacon and eggs on the bedside table.

She scrunched her brows together—breakfast food? Was it eight-thirty in the *morning?* Gasping, she rushed to the window and peered outside to see the sun rising in the east. At first, she thought she'd slept only a few hours, but she'd slept through the night.

Oh... Maya scraped her hands through her hair and pressed her palms against her eyes. She'd stayed here too long already, and had to keep moving. Had to somehow get off this island to some place much safer. Her stomach growled, clueing her in to her voracious hunger. More than twenty-four hours had gone by since she'd had a decent meal.

The eggs and bacon made her mouth water. Cheryl must have brought it in some time this morning and left it for when she woke up. Or had Connor entered the room, hoping she was ready to give him answers?

Then Maya spotted the cell, sitting next to the plate along with a note that read, *Make your calls, then we'll talk.—Connor.*

He trusted her enough to leave his phone. Maya warmed at the gesture. Yesterday, she'd been desperate for his help and had agreed to go with him, ending up here at Cheryl's house. Today, she needed to break from him, from his brother, or both of them—and now Cheryl and Karen—would be hurt because of her. But she also had to convince Connor to let go of the Learjet.

How could she make any of that happen? She'd never felt so helpless, and despite her night of sleep she still felt exhausted. Nerves and fear worked against her, polluting her mind with hopelessness.

Devouring the food, she finished the juice, counting on the nourishment to change her state of mind. Slowly, she reached for the phone and slid her sweaty palm around it then squeezed, dreading the call to her mother.

She still blamed the woman, an American, for marrying her father, a Colombian drug lord. Maya lay back on the bed and stared at the ceiling, pressing down the unbidden memories. Her mother had waited until Maya was kidnapped as a child before she opened her eyes to the truth. Finally she fled the country, returning to the U.S. to raise her daughter.

Maya had made the next mistake.

Gripping Connor's cell, she called her mother, who expected her to stay in touch, calling her every day on her risky venture into Central America. It was doubtful she even knew that Maya had been kidnapped by Roberto again. If her mother had called and left a message, she would be worried if Maya hadn't called her back.

Her mother answered on the first ring.

"Mom," Maya said. "It's me."

Immediately her mother fell into hysterics, rattling off about the kidnapping.

"Calm down. How…how did you know?"

"Your father." She sniffled and drew in a breath. "He contacted me and told me what happened."

So Roberto had informed her father that he'd kidnapped her. What else had he told him? Did he even know his men had lost her yet? Or that his jet had been taken from him? Maya didn't doubt that he did, considering the fighter jet that had tried to intercept them.

"I wanted you to know that I'm okay." For now.

"You'll never be safe until the man who kidnapped you is dead. You should never have gone to meet your father." Her mother fell into more sobs.

"Mom, I need his number. It's in my cell phone and they took it."

"Where are you now? How did you get away?"

The less her mother knew the better for everyone, especially Connor and his brother and friends. "Give me his number. I need answers."

"Just get home. Do you need me to wire you the money?"

Though she hoped they would never need to use their emergency plan, she and her mother had put measures in place in case the worst happened.

"I'm not sure. I'll get back to you if I can't get money from a bank." If there was a branch of her bank on the island then with her passport she might be able to withdraw funds. "Now, the number."

After her mother told her the number where she could reach her father, she said her goodbyes, reassuring her mother she would be home soon. She knew they both needed to hear the words, whether they believed them or not. It was all either of them had.

Maya paced the small room, thinking through her next call. Though she hadn't allowed herself to cry in years, the burning behind her eyes intensified, and she feared she'd fall apart on the phone with him. She needed to gain control over her emotions before speaking to him.

But how did she get that? Through levity? Peace? Prayer?

This was the phone call of her life.

Rap, rap, rap.

The knock at the door startled her. Maya stilled, knowing Connor was on the other side wanting answers she wasn't ready to give. Her throat constricted—the time had come to tell him everything he wanted to know, though she'd hoped to avoid this moment.

She swallowed, realizing how much she wanted—no, needed—to confide in someone. To confide in him.

Seeing his face would go a long way in bringing her a measure of comfort. That in turn could restore the composure she needed to make the phone call to her father.

But answering his questions—nausea swirled in her stomach at the thought of it.

Rap, rap, rap. "Maya?"

The sound of his voice increased her anxiety, but she opened the door. The sturdy pilot filled the doorframe, his expression stern, at first, sending a jolt of dread through her heart. It wasn't what she'd hoped for.

Then…slowly…the frown between his brows softened, and his lips transformed into a kind, reassuring smile. "Come here," he said, his voice tender. Affectionate.

Though wary, how could she resist this man? She considered herself strong, but even strong people needed a comforting hug, or at least that's how she justified her staggered step forward.

Strong arms wrapped around her as though sweeping her away from all her troubles. She pressed her face into his broad chest as if it was the most natural thing in the world. If only they could have met under different circumstances, she knew they would have been good together. Was there any hope she'd get her chance to know him if she survived this? Doubtful, once he learned the truth.

In his arms, she could feel the athletic build she'd already admired, but he was more than just ruggedly handsome. He was gentle and caring, and it hadn't taken her long to figure that out. Anyone else would have quickly turned her over to the authorities and been done with her.

But not Connor.

Now if only she could be certain he would still be there for her when all her secrets were revealed….

"The Learjet will take another week and a half to repair." Connor's breath warmed her ear. "I'm happy to fly you home, but I'm not sure what we're up against here, or if we can wait that long. You need to tell me everything. I can't help if you don't."

Nor could he help himself if he didn't leave her alone, leave Roberto's Learjet behind.

Maya snuggled deeper, wanting to block out the nightmare. In his arms, she felt safe. He was a man without fear. In that way, he reminded her of her father—at least the good memories she had of him before she'd been kidnapped the first time. Before she'd learned the truth about him. Before her mother had taken her away.

To her disappointment, the pilot relinquished his hold and eased away. He lifted her chin, forcing Maya to look into his intense gaze. Gold flecks sprinkled his blue irises—she hadn't been close enough to see that before.

The same concern she'd seen earlier filled his eyes, reminding her that he cared. As if she could forget what he'd already done for her.

Then his gaze drifted over her face and stalled at her lips.

The overwhelming sense that he wanted to kiss her wrapped around her. Her pulsed jumped to her throat.

Drawn to this man, the desire to respond and kiss him back tugged at her, luring her out of hiding. It was much too soon. She didn't know him, and even if she did—Maya had loved before and been burned. First by her father, and then by a man she thought she loved. A man she thought returned that love.

Don't trust him. Remember Eric. And when Connor learns the truth...

In the end, men could not be trusted.

TEN

Swine....

That's all he was. Connor silently berated himself as he reined in his sudden desire to wrap her in his arms again and kiss her thoroughly.

Maya's presence did crazy things to him. When her warmth had pressed against him, and she'd hugged him as if her life depended on it, Connor could hardly remember why he'd come to her room. She needed him.

How long had it been since anyone had wanted him, much less needed him?

But he didn't want to be as his brother had been, loving women and leaving them. Taking advantage of them when they were in vulnerable situations. To be fair, Jake had said he'd changed and Connor believed him, but Connor had seen the damage Jake had left in his wake before.

Still, this was something much more. Connor found his deep sense of protectiveness stirred when it came to Maya. He'd knocked on her door fully prepared to drag every morsel of truth from her. After Jake had spent hours last night chewing him out for their current state of affairs and his inability to take control, Connor knew he had to find out the facts or Jake would take matters into his own hands.

Connor couldn't allow that to happen. This situation belonged to him alone. He had to own it, or he would forever be a failure, and if the outcome was anything but positive, he would stay that way.

But when he'd seen the unfathomable pain lurking behind her tired eyes—beautiful, thoughtful eyes—his steel composure melted away. He hadn't planned for his reaction. If he knew for certain they were off the grid and safe, he could relax a little. Give her some time. Give *them* some time.

What was he thinking?

I've lost it. Really lost it this time.

He stood close enough now that her honey-and-vanilla scent enveloped him, enticing him. Connor had to shake free of her essence and the power it had over him now.

He took a step back, and then another, putting a safe distance between them. Her nearness had almost done him in. He'd do well to remember that he was no good when it came to relationships.

That much was clear after Darrah broke off their engagement. She couldn't take the daredevil side of his personality. Connor wasn't prepared to have his heart shattered again.

Maya watched him expectantly. So what did he say now? That he was sorry he'd almost kissed her? He was and he wasn't.

"It's time you tell me everything. I haven't called the police because you asked me not to, and because you warned me not to trust anyone. I want to know why."

She turned her back to him. "We need to go our separate ways now. That's for the best."

Her words drove him crazy. "Do you have money and a way to get to safety? Have you made that phone call you wanted to make?"

She shook her head, her silky long tresses swaying against the middle of her back. Connor wanted to reach out and run his fingers through them. He drew in a breath to clear his head.

"You should get some fresh air and make the call." He paused, giving her a chance to reply, but when she didn't, he squeezed her shoulder. "They have a wrap-around deck in the back. You can see the beach. Let's sit out there."

Finally, she turned to face him and nodded. "I'd like that."

Connor held his hand out, just as he'd done at the airport. What was with him and this woman? She half smiled, half frowned and stared at his hand. He saw how difficult it was for her to trust, and he wanted to know why. He wanted to know everything about her.

Instead of taking his hand, she grabbed his phone from the table. "I need to call my father, and then I can tell you what you need to know."

Connor led her out of the room and down the hallway. He didn't know why her words troubled him. He hoped her father was someone who could help her but the way she'd said it, he had a bad feeling.

A very bad feeling.

He opened the door for Maya. She hesitated and peeked outside, then stepped through the door, the morning sun highlighting the many hues in her hair. It was then he noticed she held her breath.

Connor tensed. If she was that concerned Roberto would find her here… "Maybe we shouldn't go outside."

"No, it's okay. I need fresh air, like you said." She angled her head, searching the surrounding houses that peeked through the thick foliage separating the yards, and the small strip of beach they could see from here.

Maya looked his way, obviously aware he was watching her, and tried to offer him a smile—he could tell it was forced. She made her way to the padded wicker chairs and sunk into the one with a matching stool. Connor remained standing, every ounce of his awareness focused on Maya and their surroundings.

If he could crash an F-22 Raptor and survive in the Iraqi desert, he could handle this.

Maya fiddled with his phone. *Come on, Maya. Make the call.*

He needed to know what he'd gotten into. Last night, when he and Jake had argued, Reg had come up. Neither of them wanted to call their older brother. Bridges had been burned. Reg considered Jake an irresponsible lout and Connor reckless if not a coward. The thought stung him again.

He wanted to be so much more. To prove himself. The very last thing he wanted to do was to prove his brother right, by calling Reg and asking for help. Jake agreed. They both decided they would handle this situation.

But Connor couldn't ignore the niggling that he should swallow his pride and call Reg. Unfortunately, calling him didn't equal reaching him—the man could have a new number now for one thing, even if he wasn't on an undercover assignment. And even if he reached him, talking to Reg didn't mean that he would agree to help. Connor's involvement with the kidnapping, the drug lord and the Learjet would embarrass anyone, especially Reg, an accomplished FBI agent. Not like Connor.

Always a failure, never a hero...

His back to Maya, the words tore at his insides again. A salty breeze rushed over him, nudging him from his thoughts and to Maya. When he realized she was actually making the call he turned to her. "Do you want me to leave, give you some privacy?"

She shook her head, then she spoke into the phone in Spanish. Surprise engulfed him. Tension and hot emotion spiked her words and her eyes flooded with moisture. Then her gaze bore into him. "In English, please," she said.

In that second, Connor realized she wanted him to hear this conversation, and speaking in English was for his benefit.

He would get his answers now.

A knot constricted her throat, strangling her words. She was on hold, waiting for someone to take the phone to her father. This was the man she hadn't spoken to since she was five until two weeks ago. A man she thought she was going to meet in Belize.

Connor watched and listened now, she was aware. She decided it would be easier for him to hear her conversation than for her to explain. She doubted she could accurately convey the extreme nature of this to him, even in the face of their experience together so far.

She owed him that much.

He was right—he needed to know everything. She saw that now, though she'd not wanted anyone to know her heritage. She peered into his troubled blue gaze, her heart begging him to understand as she waited for her father.

"Mi hija." The familiar voice spoke over the line. The same voice she'd heard a few days ago when he'd requested to see her before cancer took him, only this time, anguish squeezed his tone.

A sob broke through, keeping Maya from her reply. *"Papá..."* Another sob squeaked out when she called him by the endearment she'd used as a child. Maya drew in a long breath and focused her thoughts. She had to make it through this call. *"Inglés, por favor,"* she said. "In English, please."

She put the cell on Speaker.

"Of course." He sounded drained, as if…as if he was dying.

Oh, Lord, it was true. And Roberto Hernandez had kept her from seeing her father now, just as he'd done her whole life. His evil influence, along with the years, the distance and her father's chosen career, had separated her from him. The memories, thoughts of all she'd lost, now slammed her against a wall of desolation.

"Are you all right?" he asked.

"Yes, I think so. For now, anyway. I'm on an island. Golden Key."

Her father swore under his breath. Had he thought she wouldn't hear?

"Someone is helping me," she said, glancing at Connor. "What happened? Why didn't you meet me?"

"My driver was ambushed, we were delayed." Tears filled his words. "Forgive me, Maya. All I ever wanted for you was a normal life. That's why I let you go, let your mother go. I never thought he'd try to kidnap you again. I'm still trying to find out how he knew you would be there."

"Tell me—why did he try again?" Grief and dread crashed into her. "What can I do now?"

"Stay low and hidden. Hernandez has contacts on the island, and if his men aren't already there, it won't be long until they're looking for you. Let me deal with things from my end. You cannot trust anyone, including the police, until I have dealt with the matter. I will try to send help for you, but if you can, get off the island.

"Maya, listen to me." His voice turned grave. "Years ago, I was the one to start this. I kidnapped Hernandez's only son. I don't know how to tell you this other than to say the child…did not survive. Hernandez was out for revenge then. He wants you now because his cartel has been destroyed. He is a desperate man, wanting to play his last and final card against me, especially before I die."

Maya stopped breathing. She was sure her heart had stopped, too, or at least had broken, shattered into a million pieces by fear and disappointment.

In an instant, Connor was by her side, sitting next to her, cradling her as though he sensed her complete devastation, and still, she barely registered that he was there.

"Maya," her father said. He exhaled, the sound of his regret cavernous. "Maya, if I don't see you, if we never speak again before I die, please know that I love you. I never stopped loving you. I pray you forgive me. I retired from my endeavors long ago. I'm not that man anymore." She barely registered the click as the call ended.

Maya found herself burrowing deeper into Connor's arms as he rocked and soothed her broken heart. She stared at nothing, only seeing her life in Colombia. The good years. Had her father really kidnapped another man's child? *Murdered* the child?

It was too much to bear. She was both horrified and deeply saddened, even more disappointed in him than before, if possible.

If only I could start over. But my life will never be the same. "He asked me to forgive him. Told me he loved me. He's a changed man," she mumbled. But that didn't change what he was, what he had been, or what he'd done to another man's child. A man who was determined to take his revenge.

She had no hope of escape. Of survival.

Somehow she had to bury her anguish over learning the truth. But she couldn't. Stunned, she couldn't shake free from absolute despondency as it washed over her, drowning her in shock, confusing her.

"Maya," a voice whispered.

Someone lifted her and carried her now. Maya stared at the man holding her. She frowned, grasping for reality, but it was out of her reach.

"Maya." The voice belonged to the man who carried her. The pilot. Connor. He set her on a sofa and she fell back against the cushion, staring at the ceiling but seeing nothing.

Her father had murdered a child. *My father*...Papá...

Nothing she'd done with her life, nothing she could ever do, would change the fact that her father's actions from long ago had set the course for her whole life. Was even now affecting her future.

That child's father, Roberto Hernandez, would take her life to settle the score.

ELEVEN

Thank goodness Cheryl and her mother had gone out to get groceries. Connor had no idea how he would explain Maya's current state. It was as if she'd crumpled, just given up right before his eyes.

On the one hand, he didn't blame her—things were much worse than he'd thought. In fact, he couldn't have imagined this.

Maya's father is a Colombian drug lord...his enemy after her.

Or at least a retired drug lord, for whatever that was worth. From where Connor stood it wasn't worth much at all.

Rage burned inside. At himself. At Maya's father and at Maya. She should have told him sooner. He should have taken action sooner. But what action could he have taken if they didn't know who they could trust?

If what her father said was true, Hernandez had contacts on the island, and it was likely his men were already searching for her. Maya had already warned him of this possibility.

They definitely needed to stay low and hidden. They needed to get off this island and find someplace safe, forget about waiting for the Learjet.

No one was going to come to their rescue—except whoever Maya's father sent. But Connor wasn't about to take help from a wanted man.

"Here, give her this," Jake said, handing a cup of hot coffee to Connor.

He set it on the table next to the sofa where he edged next to her, and pressed his hands gently against her cheeks, turning her to face him. "Maya, look at me."

She stared at him, but she had that distant look that told him she was lost in a land of memories, or hopes and dreams of a nonexistent future. He couldn't tell which, but if he didn't pull her out now, he doubted he could. She'd never see her future or her dreams come true.

"What's wrong with her, exactly?" Jake asked. "Drugs?"

Nice tact, Jake. Connor didn't know how to answer and gave a slight shake of his head. "She's...in shock."

Connor didn't look up at Jake but could tell when his body tensed as he sat in the chair across from Maya. "Want to share the news with me?"

"Not now." Connor cut his brother a look. *Later...*

He wasn't sure what to do for her, but he had to try. She seemed to care that he and Jake were safe and had suggested they leave her to her fate. After what he'd just heard, he was even more determined to stick with her despite her protests. No way would he leave her to face this alone.

He gripped her arms and lifted her, gently shaking her, and pressed his face near hers. "Maya, come on. We have to find a safe place to stay. All of us. We have to leave Cheryl and her mother or they could be in danger."

He shook her again, gently. She slipped from his hands and curled into a ball on the sofa, squeezing her eyes. Good. She'd heard him. That was a step in the right direction.

Gripping her waist and supporting her head, he forced her to sit up. He took the coffee and pressed it to her lips, but she wouldn't drink. Instead her eyes remained closed, a desperate, pained expression on her face.

"Listen to me. This isn't who you are. You're stronger than this. I need you to be strong right now." He couldn't sit here and watch her allow what was apparently a lifetime of repressed resentment and grief destroy her. "Our lives depend on you being strong."

Maya finally opened her eyes to look at him. Tears streamed down her cheeks, and she swiped them away. "I'm sorry. You're right except for one thing. Your life doesn't depend on me. It depends on you getting far away. And I need to get out of here."

Maya stood but swayed on her feet and Connor steadied her. "I'm not leaving you alone in this. How many times do I have to tell you that?" Lines creased her forehead, emphasized her confusion. By the look in her eyes, Connor knew she didn't believe he would stay the course.

Then she glanced down at her attire as if seeing what she wore for the first time—old baggy sweats and a T-shirt. "I need to get to a bank for some cash, and I need new clothes."

"I'll take you to the market we saw on the way. I want to scope out the island, assess the danger factor. We might be safer than we think, at least for a while, maybe even until the Learjet is fixed." But he didn't believe his own words.

Neither did she.

"Don't count on it," she said.

Jake bolted from his chair and threw out his hands.

"Whoa, whoa…whoa. *What* is going on? What kind of trouble are you in, Maya? I mean, Connor told me that we have a drug lord after us, but looks like things have gotten much worse when I didn't think they could."

"Jake!" Connor could punch him.

"I'll let you tell your brother while I go splash water on my face."

Connor watched her trek away from him. The look on her face sent shards of grief slicing through him. She'd transformed from a warm, though desperate, woman, to a cold hard stone. Maybe that's what she had to do in order to survive.

Maybe he should follow her example. Maybe that's what he'd need to do in order to survive, too. His brother shoved him, wrenching him from his painful thoughts.

"How bad is it?" Jake worked his jaw now.

The last thing Connor wanted was to get into this with his brother, but he had to tell him what he'd just learned.

Connor swiped a hand down his face. "You knew it was bad already. Don't act like you didn't know."

Jake angled his head. "Connor." The way his brother said his name reminded him of their father demanding respect. Demanding answers. Connor had wanted them himself and now he had them.

He paced to the window and took a peek outside, wary now of every passing car, every pedestrian walking the sidewalk. As he explained the full scope of their situation to his brother, he hoped they were safely hidden on the little island. But he'd been wrong to think that landing here had bought them time. They'd landed in the worst place. He couldn't have known, even if Maya had told him who her father was.

He'd wanted to help this woman, considered himself her protector, and he didn't even know the first thing about her. Where did she live? Why had she gone to Belize in the first place? But wait, after listening to the conversation with her father, he could guess at the answer to the last one.

She'd gone to meet her drug-lord father in Belize. Connor's stomach roiled.

"That's it, Connor. We have to call for help."

"Her father told her what she's already told us. We don't know who we can trust."

"You're going to take the word of a drug lord? Of his daughter?"

Connor heaved a sigh. "I'm not going to argue with you."

Jake sagged. "You're wrong, you know. We do know who we can trust. I didn't want to do it, but calling Reg might be our only choice."

Slumping into the chair, Connor pressed his hand over his forehead. "I can't call him. Not yet. I don't want to drag him into this, too, like I did you. I'm not sure what he could do to help us anyway." *I need a chance to fix this.*

Connor couldn't return his brother's gaze, but he could feel the tension pouring from him.

"He's not easy to reach," Jake said, his manner suddenly turning sympathetic. "Don't beat yourself up. What are the chances we could get through to him anyway, right? What are the chances he'd even take our calls?"

Jake's heavy sigh weighed on Connor. "It doesn't look like I'm going to fly that jet out of here so we can forget about waiting for it. Do what you think is best."

Feeling the regret of his mistakes to his bones, Connor waited for Jake's reaction. Jake nodded his agreement.

What was taking Maya so long? Connor left his

brother and stalked down the hallway. He knocked on the door and waited. Then he opened it.

She was gone.

Maya jogged between the bungalows, trying to keep a low profile, trying to escape Connor and his brother. Or rather, put safe distance between them. They didn't have to risk their lives for her. If they chose to stay for the Learjet, that was their problem, but she wouldn't stand by and watch either of them get hurt because of her.

She couldn't allow Connor to be her champion, after all.

The whir of a small plane resounded somewhere above. Maya ducked under an awning, hoping the homeowners or vacationers were out for the afternoon. Regardless, it wasn't likely they'd see her unless they were outside.

She couldn't live like this.

Running.

Hiding.

Lord...God in heaven...help me?

The cry came from the deepest part of her heart, as it should. Her father had been a staunch religious man, mixing his faith with his crimes, and she'd struggled to reconcile the two when she'd grown old enough to consider the life she and her mother had fled. It was impossible.

But she knew Jesus could save. That He *would* save.

He'd saved her from her sins, but now she needed Him to save her from her father's sins.

"Hey!" Hands on hips, a man stood in a wide stance a few yards away. "You. What are you doing there?"

Maya shoved from the stucco wall of the house and ran, ducking between the small bungalows and cot-

tages, dodging around vehicles, across yards and between flowering bushes and palm trees.

Finally, her breath spent, she slowed and made her
way down the sidewalk to the flea market. But should
she go there? Connor would probably look for her at
the market first—if he'd even discovered her missing
yet. Or, he could simply let her go. She'd told him repeatedly he didn't have to share her burden, and she'd
been surprised he hadn't walked away after hearing the
truth about her father. Give the news time to sink in, and
the pressure to squeeze, and Connor would break if he
hadn't already.

Trust no one.

She reminded herself of her words to Connor. She
would do well to follow them, too.

The burden was far heavier than she'd comprehended.

Her father was a murderer. But then she knew that,
didn't she? How could a person sell drugs and not kill
people either directly or indirectly?

Since her conversation with him, the weight she carried had grown exponentially heavier. She couldn't have
prepared for this news.

Her father had killed Roberto Hernandez's only child.

His only child.

My father's blood runs in my veins. Did that make
her guilty, too?

"No," she sobbed, and yet, she was paying the price
for his misdeeds just the same. She had to hurry and
picked up her speed.

His enemy wanted to kill her. Would stop at nothing.

No matter what she did, she didn't feel as though she
could get away from him.

Just like in her nightmare.

Though unsure of where she would go, she had to get

cash and a few necessities, including clothes that fit. In order to lay low, she needed to blend in and stay hidden, as her father had put it.

Her throat burned. Tears welled. Too many emotions accosted her at once. To complicate matters, Connor Jacobson had quickly found his way under her skin. But intense situations could often create a bond that couldn't stand up when life returned to normal, to the mundane. Facing death could work like a pressure cooker on any feelings they shared.

But normal? What was that anyway? Whatever it was, Maya doubted her life would ever return to it. She'd fooled herself into thinking she'd found ordinary to begin with. She jogged forward, the market in sight, her gaze scanning the streets for a bank, knowing she'd be taking a big risk in going inside if she found one.

Since Roberto had contacts on the island, her previous words to Connor were true, and she couldn't trust a soul. Not even a bank teller. And she'd just dumped the only help she had, the only man she could reasonably trust.

She strode across the street and into the busy market, hoping to blend in while watching for anyone who might follow her. She spotted a bank a few blocks down—just what she needed. Despite her shabby, too-big clothing, she made her way through the lobby doors and stood in line like the rest, careful not to draw more attention to herself than necessary.

While scanning a free newspaper, acting like a local, she watched the other customers, and eyed the tellers to see if anyone threw her suspicious glances. Once it was her turn at the counter, she revealed her passport and explained that her wallet had been stolen.

Cash in hand, Maya exited the side door of the bank and found herself in the alley. She scanned the street long and hard before making her way back to the market in search of something more appropriate to wear. The next thing on her agenda—figure out where she would go. What she would do.

Her father told her to keep hidden until he'd handled the situation. That he would send help. But how would she know who that was? How would he contact her? The fact remained that he hadn't managed to take care of his enemy in over twenty years. Roberto Hernandez was still his nemesis and was very much alive and well.

Very much after her.

She finally realized she couldn't count on her father to end this.

Racks of clothes were positioned on the sidewalk outside a dress shop with a large awning. It provided enough shadowy covering to make her feel moderately safe. She found a stand with shirts and another with shorts and rummaged through them. Was it too much to hope that Roberto didn't know she was here?

But she hadn't been the only one to notice the nasty smirk the CBP officer had given her. Connor had seen it, too. Regardless, sooner or later Roberto would find the Learjet—it wasn't something easily hidden. Find the plane and he would know that Maya had landed on this island with the Jacobson brothers.

She tugged out a yellow island shirt with blue flowers and some white shorts. That would do for now. Add another shirt, a pair of jeans, a hat—oh, and she spotted a money belt—and she'd be good to go. Maybe she'd wear a swimsuit underneath, just in case staying hidden meant a jump off a pier.

Dressed like this, she'd definitely blend in. That's all she could think of to keep safe at the moment. Maya held the shirt up to a mirror—not that her appearance mattered all that much but it was a simple force of habit.

Under the circumstances, her habits would need revamping.

She paid the salesclerk and changed in the dressing room, slipping on the swimsuit first and the new outfit next. Then she stuck some cash in the money belt she could wear under her clothes. Feeling more herself, Maya hung back under the awning between the racks of clothes, and peered out into the street.

What next?

An ache sliced through her. She could no longer ignore what she'd tried to dismiss since leaving Connor.

Deep inside, she'd wanted him to find her in spite of the fact that she'd skipped out on him. But he hadn't come for her, and her sense of loss was profound. She'd been right to think he would abandon her once he learned the truth.

Maya inwardly chided herself. This was for the best, wasn't it? Hadn't she repeatedly begged him to stay away from her?

The market grew busier as late morning approached early lunch, and though people—young women with children, singles, couples, island bums and preppy jocks—moved around her, Maya stayed glued to the wall of the shop, still reeling that she was alone.

Utterly alone.

When Connor was with her, his presence had wrapped her in a powerful sense of protection and safety. She'd known she'd miss that when she was on her own, but she hadn't expected her disappointment when he didn't come after her to be so deep, as if someone had carved a hole out of her heart.

Then she saw something. Some*one*. Lurking across the street.

Staring. The man threw down a cigar butt and looked away to reveal a knifelike scar. But he'd been watching her, she knew it. Felt it. And not because he was simply admiring her island shirt.

TWELVE

There...

Connor's heart slammed against his ribs. He thought he'd never find her. Discovering that she'd left him to face the drug-lord nightmare of her past alone had been like a punch to his gut.

And he'd let it happen. He'd watched her walk away from him. That cold, dead look in her eyes, the result of her resolve, should have warned him that she planned to run.

He'd failed her. But now that he'd succeeded in tracking her down, he wouldn't fail her again.

She stepped out the side door of a small dress shop, wearing a flowery shirt and shorts and a girlie baseball cap, a panicked look on her face—she must have seen the man who shadowed her, too. Then she disappeared into a bistro filled with customers. Connor entered through the front door where tables served the lunch crowd. He made his way over to peruse the offerings until he was just behind her. Her honey-vanilla scent wafted around him, even in the midst of the bistro's aroma of French and Italian breads, buttery croissants, seafood and chicken. She fidgeted with an omelet pan, acting as if she was considering a purchase.

Blending in. Hiding in plain sight.

It was no good. The fact that someone had already found her showed that her efforts were wasted.

Suddenly, she stiffened. She must have sensed his presence, sensed him watching. She made a move to run. He reached under her arm and gripped, holding her in place. She spun around to face him.

"You can't do this alone," he whispered.

Her eyes grew wide, glistening in the sunlight that spilled through the bistro windows. Relief swept over her features, and in that moment he connected with her.

His pulse slowed.

And pounded in his ears.

In that instant of time, he read her as he hadn't been able to before—she was glad to see him. Connor's pulse kicked back to normal time, and then ramped up a notch, but not because she was in trouble or someone was after her. Was after *them*.

No. His heart rate quickened for an entirely different reason. He shoved away the craziness that always overwhelmed him when he was with her. He didn't have time for this. Being with Maya was dangerous for him for more reasons than a crazed drug lord who wanted to kill her.

Connor didn't have time for romance. Couldn't risk it even if he did. His heart had already been shattered to smithereens.

Being with her and the emotions she ignited in him was a dangerous combination for them both. He needed to keep his attention focused on protecting them.

"You shouldn't have followed me." She shrugged free and turned to leave.

But she didn't mean the words—he'd already seen in her eyes how she really felt when they'd…connected.

"Maybe not, but I'm here. I'm not leaving until you're safe." Across the crowded bistro, a few patrons waiting in the doorway to be seated for lunch, Connor saw the man with the scar who'd been watching Maya before. He shoved through the crowd.

Connor gripped her arm again. "Time's up. Let's get out of here."

She didn't argue but followed him through the back of the restaurant, through the kitchen where pots and pans clanked, and chefs scowled at them. With each set of eyes that followed them, Connor wondered who would tell their pursuer which way they'd gone.

Who would readily give them away? Who was the drug lord paying to watch and call him if Maya was spotted?

Shoving through the back door of the bistro, Connor looked down the alley. First left, then right. The man was probably already running to the back of the restaurant, or around the outside and to the alley where he would expect them to exit.

"This way." Connor ran, tugging Maya behind him, but he had no clue where to go. He was living in the moment.

Living to fight another day.

With Maya's grip strong in his, he was more determined than ever to find a way to make her safe. They took a left at the corner of the building and joined the busy market again. Maya struggled to catch her breath behind him. He stopped and turned to check on her. Though she'd held on to her bag and a merchant sack, she'd lost the cap. They weren't going back to retrieve it.

Her chest rose and fell with her labored breaths. "I can't run anymore. I need to rest for a minute."

A police cruiser crept through the crowd. Connor

pressed her against the wall of a dilapidated but busy tackle shop and he hovered near, hiding her. Protecting her. Though warning sirens screamed in his head, he leaned in closer, only a few inches from her face, and lingered.

Her amazing eyes grew wide. "What…what are you doing?"

"Just go along with me. This way, we'll look like a couple enjoying a private moment." In the shadows of the awning, they wouldn't draw any attention or look suspicious.

She nodded. "Okay."

Tension corded the muscles in his neck. He didn't dare look behind him to see what was happening. Instead, he willed her to be safe, focused on shielding her.

Her gaze studied his shirt, avoiding his face. His eyes.

"This is going to work. Don't worry." He smiled, hoping to coax her into believing him.

She offered the slightest hint of a grin in return, despite the wariness flooding her gaze. Deep down in his shattered heart, in the growing soft spot he had for her, Connor knew that something was happening between them.

He was in big trouble.

In his peripheral vision, he spotted the cruiser heading away from them.

"Maya," he whispered. "Where did you think you would hide on this island? Why did you run away?"

"I don't know." She tossed her head back, her anxiety apparent, her face flush from the heat and their jaunt through the alley. "I just wanted to make you safe, figure things out on— Oh, no. Scarface. He's in the street, looking for us." She turned her face away.

Scarface? Connor guessed the nickname fit. He seized

her hand again and led her through the crowd, looking for a place to hide. The throng moved in and out around them, as if it was alive and breathing, and hopefully distancing them from their pursuer.

Connor had spent his career risking his life—both as a fighter pilot, as a test pilot—and now he was reduced to this. Running away on foot in a crowded market on an island.

The scenario hardly seemed appropriate given his experience, but he shouldn't forget his habit of destroying expensive airplanes—looked as though he wasn't changing that habit even with the Learjet. A vise squeezed his chest. That wasn't how any of this was supposed to turn out.

Then he looked at Maya and determination surged inside. He couldn't help but hope that somehow he could save the day. And he would save it, if given half a chance.

"Where are we going?" Maya asked, her body pressed closer to his as the lunch crowd thickened.

Where did all these people come from? He didn't think the population was this big.

"I'm open for suggestions," he said, feeling like an idiot for saying it. "We need to get off this island. Maybe I could somehow get us on one of the charter flights or secure one of the private jets. There has to be someone leaving the island who would give us a ride for the right price. Then again, figuring out who we can trust hasn't changed in our favor much."

"Why not drive?"

Connor turned to face Maya, an adorable, curious smile on her face that caught him off guard. Seriously?

He tugged her to a place behind a hot-dog vendor, watching for their shadow. Looked as though they'd lost him for now.

"What do you mean drive?" He grinned, responding to the levity her teasing smile had injected into their situation. This was a side to her he'd yet to see, but they both desperately needed it, even in the face of very bad timing. "What fun would that be?"

"I'm sorry, I…shouldn't have… I can't joke around at a time like this." She averted her eyes, the lighthearted moment gone.

"Even if I agreed to drive instead of fly—" Connor peered down at her "—this island is remote. It's not connected by the Overseas Highway like the other Keys. We can't drive our way out of this." Though taking a boat—one that could handle the distance—was another option. Jake was the expert on that.

"Oh." A questioning, surprised look came into her big brown eyes. "I can't believe I didn't know that."

"Why would you, unless you've been to the Keys— or specifically to Golden Key?"

He wanted to weave his hands through her stunning length of thick, dark hair. What was the matter with him? He was doing a lousy job protecting what was left of his heart, that's what. Standing with her now, he admitted if she ever revealed she had an interest in him, he wasn't all that sure he would be able to resist getting involved, no matter his resolve to the contrary. The realization was sobering.

He swallowed to moisten his dry, thirsty mouth. Ignoring the distress signals, he allowed himself to hope just for a moment. What would it feel like to have that chance with her—a chance for something that would last? The promise of a future…

Connor's stomach leaped into his throat as if he'd jumped from a plane. Oh, he'd jumped all right—more like taken a ten-thousand-foot dive without a chute.

What was he thinking? Rubbing the back of his neck, he looked away from her sweet lips. He needed to get his focus back on keeping her safe, otherwise he was putting them both in danger.

When he glanced back at her, she stared up at him, her face a mixture of exhaustion, dread and—hope? He already knew she needed him, that she'd been glad to see him, but the way she looked at him now, it seemed as though her need had grown into something more. He could almost believe she was counting on him.

A thick lump grew in his throat. That was something he hadn't expected. But then as quickly as the emotion appeared in her eyes, it disappeared and an emotion he couldn't read replaced it. Great. Now he was back to not being able to read her.

She gazed down at her shirt and brushed away imaginary dirt. "I need to ask you something."

That sounded a little ominous, though it was hard to measure against the current state of affairs. "Go ahead."

"Did you call the police when I ran away from the house?"

"No."

"Did your brother?"

That wasn't something Connor could answer. "Jake said he would try to get hold of our older brother, Reg, who is an FBI agent. We know we can trust him, even if we can't trust the police here."

Maya's brows drew together. "And you are willing to risk his life?"

"Come on, Maya. He deals with bad guys every day. It's his job. He's well trained. The problem is he works undercover and he's difficult to reach sometimes. Most times, actually." He wouldn't bring up they hadn't spoken in two years.

"That man who is following me…"

"The one you called Scarface?"

"Yes. I saw him talk to a policeman earlier. After I went to the bank. He leaned into the window of the cruiser. At the time, I didn't think anything about it, not until after I saw him watching me. I think someone tipped him off to my presence."

"Will you listen to yourself? Your father already told you that Hernandez's men will be looking for you. To stay hidden. And what did you go and do? You left the house, a place you could have hidden, and now we're in the streets where anyone can see us. We have to believe at this point they know you're here. Could have happened when we landed. Maybe someone—the mechanic or that CBP officer—recognized his Learjet."

"I can't trust you, Connor."

"What are you talking about? Of course you can. I thought we'd already gone past this whole trust thing." This woman was trying his patience, driving him crazy.

"If I can't trust your brother, I can't trust you."

Her words pierced him because he understood—while he trusted Jake with his life, he wasn't one hundred percent sure he trusted Jake with Maya's life.

"I need to disappear without anyone, not even your brother the FBI agent, knowing my true identity. It's too bad that Jake knows, but please, make him understand it needs to remain a secret. Roberto Hernandez wants me so he can use me to get to my father. Even if they're not corrupt enough to sell me out to Hernandez directly, the authorities will treat me no differently. They will use me to get to my father. My life will not be my own."

Was she serious? How could she think that? Connor opened his mouth to reply but… Could there be any truth to her words?

She stalked away from him. Away from the throng.

"Maya, no…" He wouldn't let her do this alone. She needed help whether she was ready to admit that or not. Whether she believed she could trust him or not. If he could protect them until somehow Reg found them or sent someone to help. Or if he could get her off this island.

Scarface stepped from the shadows and grabbed her, covering her mouth with a cloth. Connor lunged for her. But the man aimed a gun at Connor and fired. Connor dodged behind a stack of crates.

If only he'd kept the Glock with him!

Ping.

Ping, ping.

The crate shielded him from three more shots.

Connor had no intention of letting the man get away with Maya. He rose from where he'd crouched, intending on pursuit. A noise above and behind drew his attention. He swung around to face the new threat.

A crate fell forward and crashed into him. Pain stabbed his head.

Darkness edged his vision until it engulfed him.

Head pounding, Maya opened her eyes to bright sunlight streaming from a skylight directly above. She squinted and rolled her head to the side. The movement didn't improve the throbbing in her temples.

Where was she? From the small bed where she lay, she could see a kitchenette, and a table with plush seating accented in cerulean. The bed rocked subtly, telling her she must be on a boat. If she had to guess, she'd say it was still in the dock, perhaps tied securely in a boat slip. Had her abductor already delivered her to his intended destination, or could she expect a boating excursion ahead to bring her to Roberto?

Her hands and ankles were bound and tape covered her mouth. Again.

This was getting old. At least this time she hadn't been locked in a small, dark lavatory. But what difference did the setting make?

None.

She closed her eyes. No matter what, she'd ended up in the same predicament—drugged for starters, and stowed away, even if this time it was in a boat instead of a plane. What was it with these guys and drugging her anyway?

At the moment, she was alone in the cabin, and she doubted whoever had taken her—had it been Scarface?—knew their drug had worn off already. Maybe she was developing tolerance. Was that her lame attempt at humor?

But there wasn't anything funny about the fact she couldn't exactly swim away with bound ankles and wrists, nor could she call for help. Her abductor knew that. She concentrated, trying to remember what had happened.

The last thing she recalled, everything turned blurry then dark but somewhere in the distance, she'd heard gunshots. She remembered that clearly.

Her heart skipped a beat—was Connor all right? Had he been hurt?

She couldn't stand the thought of him getting shot, injured—or worse, killed. She wouldn't think like that. But if he was alive, why hadn't he come for her? Why had he let someone take her?

Expecting Connor to rescue her—to be her champion—was expecting too much. No one could stand up to Roberto Hernandez or his henchmen. Not even her father. That was why she'd thrown his help back in his face. The fear that she couldn't trust his brother was only part of it. Still, she knew she'd been an idiot to walk away from him like that. She'd wanted to protect him, but if her memory of gunshots was accurate, he could have gotten hurt anyway. It had just been a dream—a fantasy—that she could have someone who wouldn't hurt her and who she wouldn't hurt.

Dream or fantasy it didn't matter—in walking away from Connor she'd given Roberto's men a chance to take her again and she still hadn't been able to keep Connor from getting caught in the cross fire.

She wanted to give up. Let it come to an end. She'd almost given up after the devastating conversation with her father. But Connor hadn't allowed her the luxury of despair, even after learning the truth about her.

Could he really believe in her?

If he were here, he would tell her that she was stronger than this, and he would drag her from the dark abyss she'd fallen into. He wouldn't let her quit now.

Her heart warmed at the thought, at the image of his face when he'd stood near her, hiding and protecting her from the cruiser in the market.

For his sake she would be strong if only for a little longer. She turned her thoughts to escaping so that she could find Connor and make sure he was all right. Thinking about saving someone else for a change felt good and right.

She scrutinized the small cabin so she could strategize an escape plan, if possible. She didn't see her bag or the sack of clothes she'd purchased, and had no idea if her items were stashed somewhere or tossed. At least she could feel the money belt still fastened beneath her shorts. Hopefully, it still contained cash.

Heavy footfalls resounded on the deck above. A door opened and someone descended the steps. Maya shut her eyes. Let her captor think she was still lost in a drug-induced unconsciousness.

The footsteps grew louder.

Someone entered the cabin, breathing hard. One of Roberto's men if not the drug lord himself. Panic threatened to strangle her. But Maya forced herself to relax, hoping she wouldn't twitch or give herself away. A soft shadow fell over her as someone thrust a face in hers, hot, foul breath blasting her cheeks.

Don't gag.

Don't flinch.

If she did either, her ruse would be up and she could forget about strategizing for an escape.

What was planned for her when she woke up? What would be done to her if she continued to sleep? The questions were agonizing and endless. But no matter what torture came, she knew she would live long enough for Roberto to look her in the eyes just before he killed her. How could she ever be free from the man?

One dilemma at a time—she needed to escape this boat.

Jesus, help me fool this person. Help me escape his attention. This boat.

The brute ran his thick calloused finger down her cheek and then ran his hands through her hair. She could imagine what he was thinking. But, no. She had to slow her pulse, remain calm, or he would see. He would know she was awake, and she'd imagine that's what he wanted—to see if she was awake or would stir.

Oh, Connor. I'm sorry I was afraid to trust you, regardless of your brother. I'm sorry I walked away.

She'd give anything now to have simply stayed by his side.

The man lifted her head. Would he kiss her while he thought she was unconscious? Maya's pulse mounted, despite her efforts.

I can't take much more of this!

If her ankles weren't bound, she'd kick him in the groin, but then again, she didn't have any hope of running away from him. Her efforts would be wasted.

A cell phone rang. The man dropped Maya's head. Pain sliced through her already pounding skull. The call had drawn his attention away, but she feared it would also seal her fate. Was it Roberto delivering instructions?

Tears surged in her eyes.

Though the man sounded distant, as though he had his back to her while he talked, if he turned around he would see the moisture streaking her cheeks. Chances were good he would have his fun with her before delivering her to Roberto.

If she managed to escape this cabin how would she get off the boat? Jumping into the water wasn't an option—she'd drown unless she could free her hands and ankles. Still, maybe that was a better fate. The man climbed the steps and left her alone in the cabin again. This time she tried to sit up, but quickly discovered her wrists bound behind her back were anchored to something.

Now she understood why there hadn't been any concern she would escape when she was left alone. He would take her to Roberto, where Connor would never find her if he was even looking, and there wasn't anything she could do. Maya closed her eyes and prayed.

The sun seemed to beam directly in on her from the skylight. She wished she could at least slide to the other side of the bed.

Minutes passed—time ushered her forward to meet her fate. In the quiet of the cabin, she heard the boat's motor start then idle. A door opened and someone descended the steps, coming for her this time, no doubt. But wait—the cadence was different; the footfalls much softer, as someone crept across the floor.

Again a shadow fell over her face and blocked the sun. She breathed calmly and slowly as if asleep. Water dripped against her face and body from whomever stood over her now.

Maya wanted to open her eyes, but she couldn't risk it. A hand gently cradled her head, and her pulse drummed in her ears.

"Maya," a gentle voice whispered. *Connor's* voice.

THIRTEEN

Maya's lids flew open, revealing the deep pools of her stunning eyes.

Connor's heart leaped into his throat.

She's conscious!

"Maya..." He peeled the tape from her mouth and gathered her into his arms. He'd intended to give her a quick, reassuring hug, except he didn't want to let her go. Not ever. "I'm so glad I found you," he whispered in her ear.

Squeezing her to him, he reminded himself they had to hurry if they were to escape. He released her and thumbed away the tear streaks.

Her eyes grew wide, drawing him into their striking depths for a half second—but urgency kicked him back to the moment and his senses.

He'd feared he'd have to swim with her unconscious weight, but more importantly she was alive, and by all appearances, unharmed, though she had to be suffering both mentally and emotionally.

Hopefully, she would be more eager to cooperate now.

"You found me!" She stared at him. "But how? How did you get on this boat? Did—"

He pressed a finger to her lips then held up a diver's

knife in his right hand, and lifted the snorkel and mask in the other. "I'll explain later," he said, his words barely audible. "But we have to hurry. Your guardian left you unattended to talk to someone on the dock. We have seconds, if that."

He was so thankful he'd been given this chance, otherwise he would have had to take her by force. He didn't relish the thought of engaging the brute Scarface had left her with.

They could hide in the water for a while, if needed, with a few accessories. Better to hide than take another vehicle affiliated with Hernandez—been there, done that and it was too big of a risk considering how many people might recognize the boat.

With quick skill, he sliced through the nylon marine rope securing her wrists and ankles, and then the one anchoring her to the bed. Quietly, he led her up the steps and hesitated near the deck, watching.

The guy stood on the dock a few yards from the thirty-foot cruiser where he kept Maya, still talking to a scrawny-looking fisherman. But Connor could barely see him from here with all the neighboring slips securing boats of every type and size obscuring the line of sight. He and Maya had a chance and they would take it.

Connor continued up and, once on the deck, he crept to the side and climbed over into the warm water, gesturing for Maya to do the same. She slid in next to him without making a splash. Even if the man had seen them trying to escape, Connor would have jumped with her and made a swim for it. But this way, they had some time to swim away between the boats and hide.

When the man realized Maya was missing, his next thought would be to search the dock. But Connor and Maya wouldn't be there.

Scarface's biggest mistake? Leaving Connor alive. Under no circumstances would he give up on finding Maya. Nor would he give up until she was safe. Somehow, he had to convince her of that.

Clinging to the side of the cruiser, Connor offered Maya a snorkel and mask.

"Wait," she said and began removing her shirt, revealing the turquoise swimsuit she wore underneath. She slipped off her sandals, as well, but left her shorts on.

Connor had quickly made the change into shorts and a T-shirt when he came up with this idea because swimming in jeans would be cumbersome, and would draw too much attention if anyone noticed. When he'd discovered Maya missing, he and Jake agreed that he would find Maya and they would hide until they could all reconnect, while Jake tried to get help, or secure a way off the island.

Apparently, Maya had thought ahead, as well, considering she wore a swimsuit, too. He handed her the mask and snorkel. This way, they'd look like a couple snorkeling, not two people hiding from dangerous men.

When she'd secured the gear, Connor took a breath and submerged, counting on Maya to follow him. Mindful of the boats, he swam deeper until he reached near the sandy bottom of the marina and glanced up. Silhouettes of watercraft hulls floated above them.

Still holding her shoes and bright shirt, Maya signaled anyone who might look for them. Connor took the clothes from her and secured the flag that was her shirt and shoes under a couple of rocks, then covered them with sand. Swimming away, he sliced through the warm water and remained as deep as he could, Maya by his side.

He hedged toward the end of the marina and the last

pier in the dock where they could lurk in the shadows and be safe from the boats. His lungs burned and he glanced at Maya. She had already started up.

But just when she reached the surface, she allowed her snorkel to breathe for her, never breaching her head above the water. Connor did the same and then he motioned for her to follow. She gave him the thumbs-up. He closed the distance that remained between them and the pier. Once in the shadows, he grabbed a post supporting the pier and broke the surface.

Maya's face pushed from the water and she shoved her mask on top of her head, along with the snorkel. Water slid over her smooth skin and slicked her hair back.

Beautiful.

Though it was difficult to pull his gaze from her, he tried to find the boat slip along the dock where the cruiser was parked. Was Maya's watchdog still talking, or had he discovered her missing yet?

There! Connor spotted him scanning the dock and the market with binoculars. Ducking a little lower in the water, Connor pulled Maya behind a thick post, though he doubted the man would think to look for them here.

"We should be safe for a minute," he said.

Gratitude played across her features. "How did you find me?"

Water sloshed around them and boards popped as people strolled above them on the pier. When Connor had come to, he'd done the only thing he could and ran down the alley where he'd seen Scarface take Maya and that led him to the marina.

"From a distance, I saw Scarface on the boat talking to a man who looked like a bouncer. I didn't know for sure, but I hoped and prayed I'd find you on the boat and that I wouldn't get there too late. That was the only place I knew to look, and it was a start at least. When I passed a booth selling snorkeling gear I thought to grab a few essentials, except I didn't grab flippers. I made a quick change into shorts, making up the plan as I went."

"Oh, Connor…" She shook her head, her eyes pouring more appreciation than he could handle. "I don't know how to thank you."

Maya drew closer, her face and lips mere inches from his. Connor's breath caught in his throat. Should he meet her the rest of the way?

Edging closer, aware only of the stunning woman before him, he lifted her chin and gently pressed his lips against hers, savoring the sweetness, the tenderness.

That she'd wanted the kiss surprised him, but he knew their actions were born from extreme circumstances. That didn't keep him from responding, losing himself in the moment. Water lapped around them, stirring his senses.

What was he doing? This wasn't the time or the place. His resolve to guard that soft spot in his heart for her, keep it from growing bigger, slowly slipped away, almost completely out of his grasp.

He wrapped his free hand around her neck, pressing her face closer, pushing the kiss deeper. Wanting her to know he returned her affection.

Still, though he might hope this kiss was sincere, that it was a promise of something more between them, he knew that hope was flimsy at best. He'd rescued her from her captors twice. She was grateful, and thought he was a hero. She was wrong.

Abruptly, she broke away. "Connor…I'm…" She averted her gaze, then her regret-filled eyes turned back on him. "I'm sorry."

"You don't have to apologize."

He lifted his hand and ran his thumb down her jawline.

Studying him, her gaze roamed his face and lips and finally lingered on his eyes. "When Scarface took me, I heard gunshots. I thought something had happened to you. I wanted to get free just so I could find you and make sure you were all right, but I couldn't. Then I decided I couldn't count on you to help me again because—"

So she *had* realized she couldn't count on him. She wanted to get away from her past for obvious reasons, and probably wasn't interested in a life with a daredevil pilot, either. But all of that could be dealt with another time.

"Shh. Shh…come here," he said and drew her trembling form into his arms.

Her frantic rambling was a bad sign.

Though they'd only been in each other's company a short time, he'd known her long enough to know she might appear vulnerable, but she was stronger than he was, given what she'd been through already. And now he had to be strong for her.

He admired her perseverance.

Somehow Connor had to pull his attention from this beautiful woman in his arms. He needed to direct all his energy to escaping Hernandez, to surviving.

When she'd calmed down, Connor released her.

She raised a brow. "You still making up the plan as you go?"

"We need to get off this island, one way or the other, but I can't leave Jake behind. I need to contact him. Find out if he got us any help. Unless you have a better idea." He tugged his cell from his pocket and held it up dripping wet. "Wasn't thinking through the plan very well, was I?"

"Look there." Maya raised her chin.

Connor peered over his shoulder at the marina near the shop fronts and the market. A police cruiser with flashing lights was parked at the curb. Were the police looking for them? Or was the cruiser there for something completely unrelated?

When he glanced back to Maya, her lips were flat, her expression grim.

"Like I said, I wasn't thinking through the plan very well," he said.

"Don't say that. You did great. I'm here, aren't I? I'm sure whatever you have in mind for our next step will get us closer to safety."

"You don't know me that well." He hated hearing the truth of those words. "Not yet, anyway."

There. He'd tossed the slim chance of a future into their fragile friendship.

Could Maya be reading his meaning wrong? Was he seriously thinking about keeping in touch with her after this was over?

That would never work—Maya couldn't see how she'd ever be free from Roberto.

She shook her head. "How am I ever going to get my life back?"

She looked away from Connor's questioning eyes. If only she could imagine a way to survive and live a normal life.

He gripped her arm, and urged her to face him, but she fought him.

"No, leave me alone. You shouldn't be here with me now. You shouldn't have come."

"You would rather I left you in that boat? In the hands

of Roberto's bouncer and Scarface planning to take you to Roberto?"

No, she hadn't wanted that, either. Without answering, she watched the marina, market and cruiser. The cop had parked and was nowhere to be seen. Oh, wait... there. He was searching for someone. From this distance she could tell he was the same policeman that her stalker Scarface had been talking to. She had no reason to think the cop wasn't working with him for Roberto.

"Look at me..." Connor tugged harder now. "Look at me."

Salt water lapped into her mouth, sloshed there by the wake of a passing boat. Maya just wanted to swim away, but she couldn't.

Slowly, she turned to face him. "I just don't want you to get hurt. I couldn't live with that. But I don't see a way out of this without someone getting injured or even killed."

His blue eyes bore into hers.

"Why are you helping me?" Especially after learning the truth about her heritage.

"Don't forget that this man is after me, too, for taking you *and* his plane. In that way, we're tied together."

Of course.

That was the only reason he was here and nothing more. He couldn't possibly care for her, despite his kiss or the concern bordering on affection she'd seen in his eyes.

His hair looked much darker now that it was wet, and the Caribbean-blue of his eyes was stark against his sun-kissed skin. Before she realized what she was doing, she reached up and ran her fingers down his face, feeling the start of a beard on his strong jaw.

He caught her wrist, and squeezed as if her touch

had cut him. Studying her, he searched her face for an-swers she didn't have. "We are getting out of this alive and together. One way or another, Roberto is going to face justice," he said.

Maya wanted to believe him. Behind them, another motor started and he released her wrist.

Connor whipped his head around to watch as the man who'd been charged with guarding Maya steered the boat from the marina. Was Scarface with him? Had they given up at finding Maya in the marina?

"Roberto will have this island locked down before we can escape," she said.

"Don't even think like that. He doesn't own this is-land."

"He doesn't have to own it." Maya tugged her mask and snorkel on and dived deep, swimming away from Connor. She'd had enough talking.

Connor swam ahead of her. Fine. Maya didn't have a problem following him for now. She had a problem with him digging himself deeper into her troubles, though.

They swam away from the pier, the marina and the market, following the shoreline from a distance. As they went, all manner of sea creatures and brightly colored tropical fish were swimming around them. A blue-and-orange stoplight parrotfish darted across her path and she paused, floating in place for a second.

Connor stopped ahead of her and turned around to discover that she was no longer following him. He mo-tioned for her to keep swimming.

She did as he asked and swam behind him, content to watch his lithe, stealthy form cut through the salty ocean. When they neared the beach, he lifted his head from the water, as did Maya.

"What do you think?" he asked. "Think it's safe to go ashore here?"

Seagulls called above them. Maya shook her head. "There's a man walking the beach."

"There are lots of men, women and children on the beach. There's always going to be someone there."

"The one wearing slacks and a light jacket instead of beach gear. Smoking a cigar and…" The man tugged his jacket back to grab something from his pocket.

"And concealing a gun," Connor finished for her.

Funny how she was beginning to feel as though she was cornered even on an island in the middle of the Gulf of Mexico.

"Okay, then," he said. "We'll keep moving."

The sturdy pilot swam away from the beach and Maya followed, wondering when this nightmare would end. Her limbs were growing tired, but she didn't want to tell Connor.

Finally, he climbed onto the outcropping of a limestone coral reef several hundred yards from the beach. A small patch of sand and grass topped the surface. "Careful. The coral can scrape you pretty easily."

Maya nodded. That's all she needed to add to her drama—an infection from a coral cut.

The beach was far enough away that the man seemed small among the others who strolled the white sands. Two snorkelers on a reef among many wouldn't draw any attention.

Connor's idea was a great disguise, she'd give him that. If the man was watching for them, they were right in front of him and he didn't even know it.

"It's like a little island," Connor said. "One of several."

Maya noticed a few other snorkelers on the other reefs.

"We can rest here for a few minutes so we won't get waterlogged," he said. "But if we hear a boat, it could be someone looking for us. We have to slip under the water just to be cautious, but act natural. Agreed?"

Nodding, Maya climbed onto the warm sand, hoping the late-afternoon sun would quickly dry her wet body. She rolled on her back and closed her eyes, imagining what it would be like to have nothing to worry about.

"What would it feel like to lie on the beach without a care in the world?" She sighed.

"Hold on to that thought, Maya. You'll be there soon enough."

She sat up on her elbows and looked at Connor. "Will I? Now that I think about it, even though I lived twenty-three years in the U.S. away from Colombia, I always had this fear in the back of my mind. It never went away. I lived all these years in denial. Connor, I am the daughter of a Colombian drug lord—how can you even look at me? Stand to be with me? Why help me?"

"Who your father is doesn't have to define you." Deep in thought, Connor frowned as he studied her. "We should pray, Maya. I can't believe I didn't do this before."

Surprised rocked through her. So Connor Jacobson was a praying man. Wow. She loved that about him.

As soon as the thought crossed her mind, she pushed it away. Conscious of the dreamy setting, she couldn't exactly say it was the wrong place, but it was the wrong time to have romantic notions.

He watched her, waiting for her reply, holding his palm out to her anyway. What was he thinking?

Maya hesitated. For years now, she'd prayed that a

past not of her own making would stay far behind her, but it had resurfaced anyway. Would her prayers for safety now be in vain?

Connor's palm remained open, his offer to pray waiting on her to decide. Finally, she placed her hand in his and he squeezed, infusing her with assurance. With faith.

As he prayed out loud for their protection, for direction, the tears spilled down her cheeks, slicing through the seawater salt that had dried on her skin.

She wanted to trust him, to believe. To be free.

But trusting long enough to breathe could be dangerous to more than her life.

FOURTEEN

When Connor finished praying he kept his eyes shut and waited for Maya. She squeaked out an amen.

He opened his eyes and reached over to brush her tears away with his thumb, feeling her soft, smooth skin, then offered her the hint of a smile.

"Thank you," she said. Her voice was raspy and choked with tears. "Prayer means a lot to me."

"I saw you praying before, on the plane. I've been praying, as well. Maybe it's time we join forces." He shaded his eyes and searched the clear waters surrounding their tiny coral island. "Maybe now you'll understand that we're in this together."

With her Hispanic complexion and dark sun-dried hair, Maya was an exotic beauty—but with the prayer, it was as though she'd opened herself up to him and he could see how beautiful she was inside. That's where it really counted.

Maya was one special woman.

Protectiveness washed over Connor anew, infusing him even more now. But it clawed at his insides that he'd just met the most beautiful woman he'd ever seen, ever known—and yes, he had to admit that now—and her life was at stake. Connor didn't have any idea how to protect her. Not really. He didn't know the first thing about her except the fact her father was a drug lord and that was a little intimidating.

What if he failed to save her—a woman who'd come to mean so much to him in a short period of time?

Why did he have to be a failure? Why couldn't he be a hero like his father, like his grandfather…and yes, even his brother Reg?

"Connor?" Maya's smooth voice cut through his thoughts. "What are you thinking?"

She watched him expectantly. He wasn't about to share his fears with her.

"Come on," she said. "I haven't seen that look on your face before. It scared me."

"No reason to be scared other than the one you already know about. I'm sure that was one of many looks you haven't seen from me, Maya. We haven't known each other that long." He did well to remind himself.

She didn't reply but instead pressed her head into the white sand, her skin and hair a stark contrast, and closed her eyes. Except for the stress he could see on her face in the tight press of her mouth and slightly furrowed brows, he would have thought she was merely sunbathing.

This ordeal was exhausting her.

But it was wearing him down, too, in more ways than one. Did she have any idea what she did to him? Her exotic beauty stirred him to the core and yet, it was much more than that.

All he knew was that he had to do everything in his power to make sure she survived this. That Hernandez would never bother her again.

"With my eyes closed, I can't see your expression now, but I still want to know what you're thinking. We might not know each other well, but if I'm to trust you to

help me, I'd like to know more about you. Your family."
Then she pushed up on her elbows again and squinted at
him. "You know about my father. Tell me about yours."

Connor glanced over to the beach. The man was still
there, hanging back in the crowd, but watching and waiting. "I come from a long line of pilots. My grandfather
was a Flying Ace, and my father—"

"Excuse me." She touched his hand. "Flying Ace?"

"In the war, he shot down several enemy aircraft.
He's a hero."

"And your father?"

"Flew a fighter jet in the Air Force. Conducted bomb-
ing strikes on a terrorist facility in Libya. Saved people."

"Oh, so he's another hero," she said. "You have a
good heritage, Connor. Good blood. That makes sense."

It makes no sense. He couldn't live up to anyone's
expectations. "My father was a strong influence on my
life, but he died in a plane crash, doing what he loved."

She remained quiet for a few seconds, and he was
glad. If she was rested enough, they should try to find
another place to go ashore.

"And what about this FBI brother you mentioned? I
suppose he's a hero, too?" she asked, shading her eyes.

Connor tensed. "I get it. You're playing the psychiatrist. Or is that what you do for a living?"

This conversation was not giving him a sense of hope,
nor did he enjoy dragging up his history.

"I'll tell you everything, once you've answered my
question."

Did he really want to go there? "Reg's a good guy,
and a good agent, from what I hear. So I guess you can
say he's a hero."

"From what you hear?"

"I haven't talked to him in over two years."

Maya sat up and crossed her legs, giving him her full attention. "What happened?"

Connor frowned, reliving the argument in his mind.

Painfully aware that Maya waited for an answer, he shook his head. "I honestly don't know what started our last argument, but growing up, we were always at each other's throats, arguing all the time. Reg was valedictorian and class president. The responsible one. I didn't care much about my grades. My senior year, while Reg graduated early from Duke, I recuperated in the hospital after crashing my Camaro."

Connor shrugged.

"Go on," she said.

"After I was discharged from the Air Force, we saw each other on Easter Sunday at Mom's. Reg and I had words and the next thing you know, he told me what he really thought about me."

"I'm so sorry, Connor. But what could he have said that would leave you two so distant?"

A pang throbbed in his chest—he'd never forgotten the words. It all came down to the heroes in their family, and Reg claimed that Connor was so afraid of winning that he always set himself up to fail.

And maybe Reg had been right, and that's why the words had stung so much. But there was no longer any truth to them. After two failed careers, Connor was now scrambling to hold himself up to the standard of the Jacobson name.

"Doesn't even matter anymore."

Reg didn't know that he'd crashed the experimental plane. At least, he hadn't come to see Connor as he recovered in the hospital. Why should he? The thought gave Connor new respect for his younger brother, Jake—the guy was willing to tag along with Connor on his harebrained idea to accept a job recovering a Learjet in the heart of Belize. Jake believed in him.

"Connor, I…"

"I don't want your sympathy."

Just thought you should know that you might be counting on the wrong guy.

But he didn't say his thoughts out loud. Connor couldn't even stand to look at her. He kept his focus on the beach and the surrounding water for danger.

Why had he told her any of that? Full disclosure, maybe? He wasn't sure being that transparent at this point was the right way to go. He wouldn't be surprised if she took off the first chance she had. Darrah certainly had.

"I wasn't going to offer you my sympathy. I was going to state that your dispute with your brother sounds like a misunderstanding—both of you taking too seriously things said that neither of you meant. And yes, the two of you have held on to your pride for two years, but—"

"Maya, don't," he said, interrupting her.

She didn't finish her thought. She wanted to berate him for being foolish, for letting that much time go by. But he had other, bigger issues. "You don't see yourself the way I do, or I'm sure the way your brother Reg really sees you, despite his hurtful words."

"Are you a psychiatrist, therapist or what?" he asked, a roguish grin creeping into his lips. She could get used to that grin.

She could tell he didn't want to pursue the direction their conversation had taken, and from experience she knew that words would not be enough to convince him of what she saw in him.

She smiled. "No. I'm a life coach."

"A what?"

"I have a degree in psychology, but I'm not a thera-pist, I don't examine or diagnose. I became a life coach so I could help people figure out their career goals and accomplish them."

"Why?" he asked.

"*My* father's choice of career had affected my life in too many ways."

Maya filled her palm with sand then let it slowly spill back to the ground as if in an hourglass. How much time did she have left?

"You see, my father wasn't a hero. He was—and is—a criminal. My mother brought me to live in the States when I was young after the first kidnapping, and I've good memories of him before we left him in Colombia. Everything about when Roberto took me then is mostly a blur. Maybe I've just blocked that out."

"I'm sure the experience terrified you."

"I missed my father while growing up. I couldn't understand what happened until my mother finally ex-plained to me that he was a bad man. Learning the truth about him devastated me, but over time, I allowed it to shape the course of my life…" Maya's throat constricted, keeping her from finishing the sentence. "I didn't make such a good decision when I agreed to meet my father in Belize. But I couldn't deny his request. He has can-cer and is dying. He wanted to see me one last time."

"I'm so sorry," Connor said, his tone understanding. But did he really get it?

"That's why it pains me that a miscommunication would keep you from your brother. He isn't a criminal. He isn't someone wanted by ten countries for dealing drugs, and yet the two of you are not on speaking terms. He's your brother and you love him. What if something happens to him? Then you'd regret not making things right. Life is too short."

"You're right." He studied her. "Life *is* too short."

"So now you know everything there is to know." Going to meet her father might not have been the wisest decision she'd made, but her so-called mistake had sent her path across Connor's. She couldn't say she wasn't glad about that, but any thoughts of a romance with him after this was a pipe dream. He couldn't be interested in her now.

"Not everything." Connor stood and peered at the marina in the distance.

"What else did you want to know?"

"Where do you live? Why aren't you married? The list goes on." He asked the questions, but his attention was on something else.

She hoped they hadn't been discovered yet because she wasn't ready to run. "How do you know that I'm not married?"

"I…uh… Because you would have said something about your husband by now." He looked down at her, a pensive expression on his face. "He would try to find you, that's how. Boyfriend?"

Maya shaded her eyes and stared at Connor. "Why so interested?"

Before Connor could answer, the whir of a motor resounded in the distance, drawing near. "Let's duck under the water. Head to the bottom of this reef," he said.

Maya nodded and they dropped into the water where they quickly put on their snorkeling gear. Before going under, Connor added, "We can follow the reef down below, maybe there's even a small hole we can hide in, so take a deep breath."

Eyes bright behind her mask, Maya sucked in air, her

chest rising. Connor dived down into the clear water and swam toward the sandy bottom, following the coral. The shadow of a boat passed over them. They were nothing more than a couple of tourists snorkeling, blending in with the many other snorkelers along the reefs.

Connor found what he'd hoped for—the reef opened up forming a small O-shaped tunnel where they could hide, just in case the boaters decided to look closely at them. He was being overly cautious, he knew, but he didn't want to take any chances they'd be seen, or worse, caught.

He was glad Maya seemed to have a good set of lungs as he swam through the tunnel and lingered on the other side of the coral reef. He turned around to wait for her. She came through the tunnel after him, her hair floating around her face, framing it. Behind her, sea anemones and starfish covered the reef.

Exploring a coral reef in the Keys with an exotic woman seemed surreal, but at the same time it disguised the truth of their dangerous predicament.

Connor pointed up and Maya nodded. He swam toward the surface and, reaching it, gently breached the water. Searching the area around them, he made sure they were alone for now before he climbed back onto the grass and sand topping the small, old limestone reef that formed a tiny island. In moments, Maya was at his side.

From this distance, he could make out the armed man still watching the beach. If the man was one of Hernandez's did that mean the drug lord had enough henchmen that he could afford to have one on the beach? What about the rest of the island's beaches?

Connor scanned the length of the shoreline. If that was the case, he didn't know what to do next, but they had to keep trying. "If you're ready, we should swim farther down the shoreline and find a place we can go ashore. I need to contact my brother, and then get us out of here."

Maya nodded and once again they swam along the shoreline, disguised as snorkelers. Connor pushed them another half mile or more and when he turned to check on Maya, she wasn't behind him. He spotted her hanging on to a similar reef, waiting for him.

Connor swam toward her, feeling guilty that he'd let so much distance pass between them, but he'd wanted to make some headway, hoping that distance would gain them the freedom to go ashore without worry. Maybe he was being overly cautious, but considering that she'd been abducted twice, once while he thought he was protecting her, Connor didn't want to take any risks.

Finally he reached her, and tugged his mask off. "Are you okay?"

Maya shook her head. "I can't keep swimming like this, I'm sorry, Connor. My legs are starting to cramp."

"I'm the one who's sorry—I didn't even think to ask how you were holding up."

"I guess I'm just not in that good of shape."

He certainly couldn't tell. By all appearances she was in great condition, but they were both exhausted—the stress of their situation draining them. He searched the shore and then followed her gaze to the marina hugging the market in the distance.

"I say we wait until dusk and swim back to the market," she said. "They'll think we're long gone from there by now."

Another boat motor roared in the distance and appeared to head their way. Someone out for a day in the water, or searching for them, he couldn't know.

Without any discussion, they both dropped under the

water's surface, and this time, they didn't bother to pull on their masks and snorkels, but followed the coral down and into the tunnel. Salt water burned Connor's eyes, but he kept them open, watching the surface and waiting for the boat to go away.

He'd never felt so trapped. They couldn't go ashore here, and now they were forced to hide underwater. Maybe his grand scheme to go snorkeling had backfired, especially considering that Maya's legs had started cramping. Regardless, they had to get out of the water and soon, and he wasn't sure they should even wait until dusk as she suggested.

He wished he could rent a boat and get off this island, but he couldn't just leave. Not without Jake. He shoved aside any worry that he wouldn't reconnect with his brother. Guilt scored the fact that he was the reason Jake was involved in the first place.

Lungs burning, Connor swam to the surface again. Maya beat him there and she pushed through first, gasping for air. Any other time he'd hope the day would never end, but now as they waited for the sun to dip beyond the horizon, he'd never experienced a longer day.

If he didn't have to worry about Maya, he would have made the beach from the beginning and walked up to the armed man and slugged him, knocked him to the ground. But they were better off staying hidden. At some point, Hernandez might believe they'd escaped the island already and give up his search.

Unfortunately, Connor had a strong gut feeling that was wishful thinking.

"Let's go," he said. He slid into the warm water. This time, he had no intention of stopping long enough to make any reef their private island.

Maya frowned, but lowered herself into the water next to him. "But it's not dark enough. What are you doing?"

"I don't want to be all the way out here when it gets dark, do you?" he teased, keeping his voice light in the hopes that she wouldn't notice how strained he felt.

She stared at him, her sweet honey eyes inviting. Spending this much time with her was beginning to get to him. Water licked her shoulders, and it was all Connor could do not to wrap his arms around her waist, pull her to him and kiss her.

Again.

But he had to be stronger than that for the both of them.

A boat drew closer and idled near them before Maya or Connor had even realized it, and instantly, she recognized it as the same boat where she'd been stowed away.

Her heart drummed against her ribs. Panic sliced through her.

"Connor," she whispered, her breathing shallow. "It's him."

He gripped her wrist and held her in place, close to him. "Don't panic. Act normal. Smile and laugh."

Quickly, she forced a smile and splashed water in his face. Then swimming on her back, she distanced herself, preparing for his pretend-playful response.

"You're going to get it now." His tone teased her, but his eyes told her she'd better run. He played his part well.

She rolled her head back with a laugh and screamed, hoping she could act as well as Connor, and then dived into the water.

This way, they were simply a romantically-involved man and woman having fun and exploring the reef.

The problem was her admiration for Connor was anything but an act, and she feared her heart would be broken if she lived through this.

Would the man who'd been charged with guarding her be fooled? Heart pounding, her pulse roared in her ears as she tried to ignore the boat floating mere yards from the small coral reef where they swam.

If she was going to convince him that she wasn't the woman he was looking for, the woman he'd allowed to escape the boat, she needed to be caught up in Connor, to lose herself in the moment. Easy enough considering that being with him stirred her to life when she hadn't known she was dead, but the pressure of being watched was overwhelming.

She breached the water a few yards from the small reef and the boat. Connor came up next to her.

"Connor," she whispered. "Do you think we convinced him?"

The boat kicked into gear and sped away, the man obviously falling for the ruse that rendered Maya unrecognizable as the woman he was after.

"There's your answer," Connor said.

Unless the man knew he couldn't catch them in the water and only went back to report his discovery. Maya sighed.

With the sun shining against his back, Connor studied her. Maya wondered how much of their playfulness, their act, was part of the ruse for him, and how much was real.

"What are we going to do?" she asked. "We can't stay in the water forever." Maya swam back to their small reef, Connor following.

She held on to a rock so she wouldn't have to float tirelessly in the Gulf waters.

Connor watched her and frowned. "Come here."

Would he kiss her again? He wrapped an arm around

her waist and hoisted her closer. He combed his finger through her hair. "We're going to make it through this."

His words of reassurance alone might not have done much, but the feel of his arms around her, strong and muscular—she didn't want to leave this place of safety. Didn't want this to end. On the other hand, she was quickly falling victim to a need she'd never known— and Maya didn't want to need anyone like she was beginning to need this man.

Though Connor didn't kiss her like before, he pressed his forehead against hers. "Maya…" he said, his voice husky.

The way he'd said her name…Maya knew she'd never recover.

He cleared his throat as though his feelings reflected hers. "With Hernandez's men still searching for us, I think heading back to the market or shore before sunset is too risky, after all."

Maya nodded, though she wasn't convinced that would make any difference. What were they going to do?

"Will you trust me?" he asked.

I want to trust you, I really do…

The sting of Eric's betrayal was never far behind her, but Connor wasn't Eric. He hadn't looked at her differently upon hearing about her father.

He ran the back of his hand down her face, affection pouring from his eyes. "Are you sure there's no one else, Maya? No one from home?" His face twisted. "I still don't know where you live."

Could this man really care about her? Could his interest go deeper than protecting her and seeing her through this crisis? Again she thought he might be considering something more long-term with her, but she feared allowing herself the luxury of that thought.

"No, Connor. There's no one. At least not anymore. There was only one boyfriend who I told about my father, and he couldn't deal with it. I live in Dallas now, to answer all your questions."

"Now I understand you better. You think my finding out who your father is makes a difference. That I wouldn't want to help you. That I wouldn't feel…"

Maya searched his eyes then. *Feel what?*

"That's why you're afraid to trust me." Hurt laced his words.

"To trust anyone. Not just you, but yes, now you understand. I'm even afraid to trust myself." Maya put more distance between her and Connor, then climbed onto the sandy top of the coral outcropping. "I'm afraid that in the end, I'm like my father. His blood runs in my veins. That's my inheritance, after all."

Lines creased his forehead and between his brows. "You can't believe that."

She scoffed. "The truth requires no faith."

"Maya, we've prayed together. You're a follower of Christ, which means you're a new creation in Christ and God is your father. Remember that." His conviction overwhelmed her.

Again the tears burned behind her eyes. His words left her broken. They were truth, but she still struggled to believe them. She swiped at the tears before they accosted her cheeks and sucked in a breath.

She also struggled to believe what she was beginning to feel for Connor. Her emotions were a wreck and surely the tender kiss they'd shared, their situation—all of it working like a high-pressure melting pot, fusing their feelings for each other.

"And learning about your father isn't going to scare me off. Not now, and not when this is over." Connor drew close and smiled, something much different replacing the hurt she'd seen in his eyes seconds before. His words sent her pulse racing.

Did he really mean that? Or was he, too, setting himself up for a big fall? Maya didn't know what to say.

As they talked, the sun merged with the horizon. "I hope so, too. But I don't…" Maya looked at her surroundings, the beach, the water, anywhere but at Connor. "I don't know if I can ever give you what you want. I've been through too much already."

Connor lifted her hand to his lips and pressed it against them. He squeezed his eyes shut for a millisecond as though savoring the experience, cherishing this moment with her. The gesture touched a place deep in her heart.

Oh, how she wanted to trust him, to fall for him completely.

Too soon, he released her hand and the magic was gone. "Once we get out of this, I hope you'll give me a chance to earn your trust."

And your love? He didn't say it—it was too soon. She was crazy to hope that he would think the words.

She was afraid to respond or give him any hope that she'd be able to completely trust him. Instead she averted her gaze, watching the nearby beach. With everything in her she began to hope that Connor would be her champion after all, that he would be the person to change everything for her, if she couldn't do it herself.

"We should go now," he said. He tugged his mask and snorkel back in place, though with dusk fast approaching, Maya doubted he could see a thing underwater.

Connor swam ahead of her and back toward the pier they'd left hours ago. His plan to hide as snorkelers had been unique and had definitely worked for them so far but had Roberto's men truly believed she and Connor and his brother were no longer on the island? Had they finally called off the search?

They'd find out soon enough when they made it to the marina, climbed onto the dock or the beach and walked through the market. But where would they go?

With so many boats in the marina, Maya wished they could rent one or pay someone to take them away. She wondered if that was part of Connor's plan or if he still expected to recover his Learjet, return it to wherever he was supposed to and get paid for it. He hadn't exactly shared his plans for their escape, but she realized that both of them were living moment by moment as they tried to stay low and hidden as her father had told her, though she'd long ago stopped counting on her father's ability to help her now.

By the time they reached the pier, the water had grown completely dark, and Maya was ready to get out. Connor didn't swim all the way to the dock and instead headed toward the shore in the shadows between the beams of the pier.

Following Connor, she thought about how they'd shared their stories and gone straight to the heart of who they were. She felt more connected to him than she'd ever felt to anyone.

Finally, he stood, water dripping from his well-defined body as the bright moonlight reflected and accented every sculpted muscle beneath his clinging shirt. Her feet on the sandy bottom, Maya rose and straightened to her full height for the first time in hours, then scraped off her mask and snorkel.

She studied the beach and the marina, expecting danger. Praying for safety. Wishing they could have been much farther away by now.

Like maybe Florida. New York wouldn't have been too far for her at this point.

The market had grown livelier with dusk, restaurants and cafés bustling with patrons. Though she hoped Roberto's men were no longer searching for them on this side of the island, or on the island at all, she feared there would be no escape, and that coming ashore wouldn't gain them anything.

Maya hung back, dreading her first step back on dry ground, though she was tired of the water and felt like a giant prune.

Connor grabbed her hand and tugged her to him as he walked. He pressed his lips to the top of her head and then leaned in to whisper. "I need to find a phone. We should keep up the act that we're a couple, okay? Even though I'm not exactly sure we've ever been considered anything else."

"I went to Belize alone, but now I think they know to look for the two of us together." Maya glanced over at the marina filled with boats.

Connor stiffened against her then paused and turned to face her, though his eyes continued to search the area, watching for any threats. Finally he looked at her, a sliver of annoyance in his eyes.

"Don't tell me you're considering running off again without me. As a couple, we're one of hundreds. Let me reiterate, just in case you have any ideas floating around in that pretty head of yours—it's not safe for you to be alone in this, especially if you're accosted by anyone."

His concern enveloped her and she offered a soft smile. "It's just that I think I'd prefer to get in a boat and leave right now than put one foot back on Golden Key."

"If I can't reach my brother, I'll leave a message and

tell him that we're taking a boat and getting off this island, all right? He can meet us in Dallas."

Maya tensed, almost wishing she hadn't told him where she was from—her old, familiar fear of trusting anyone snaking back through her with a vengeance. She'd never liked anyone knowing that much about her.

She shrugged in reply. At the moment, that was all she could give.

He's different.

He'd better be after everything she'd shared with him. After the passion he'd stirred, she counted on him more than she wanted. More than she could have thought possible. And with that, came a new dread.

She knew without a doubt that losing him would shatter her like nothing before. Did he have any idea? Did he feel remotely the same for her?

Connor frowned, apparently not too satisfied with her answer, then he started walking again, positioning himself beside her as her partner, her protector. They made the sidewalk and he pulled her into a shop where they purchased a T-shirt for him and a sundress for her along with shoes for both of them with the credit card he had in his pocket.

Different clothes would change up their appearance somewhat, but unfortunately, the shop didn't have cell phones for purchase.

When they exited the place, Connor found a pay phone at the corner of a café. He searched his pockets and, finding some coins, held them up between his fingers. "See, God is watching out for us. You never know when you're going to need change and I rarely have it. It even survived our snorkeling."

He stuck the coins in and dialed a number. Maya presumed he was contacting his brother as he'd said. She stood next to him, her back against the wall, watching the busy café entrance next to them.

Connor spoke into the phone. "Plans have changed. I don't have a working cell anymore. Since I'm leaving a message instead of talking to you, Maya and I are getting a boat and off this island. These guys have been tracking us all day, so be careful. That means you're on your own. I'll call you when I can, but find your own way out of this."

That was it—he'd done it. In order to help Maya, he'd severed the connection to his brother. Maya hoped that Roberto's men hadn't abducted Jake and were now listening to his messages, but she said nothing.

Had Connor just made a huge mistake? Guilt for what she'd done to him and his brother made her look away, her eyes scanning the crowd. Maya had stared long and hard at a man, looking him directly in the eyes before the scar on his face drew any recognition from her.

He started across the street toward them. Opening his jacket, he tugged out his gun.

FIFTEEN

Connor noticed Scarface approaching just in time, and yanked Maya around the corner. A bullet whizzed by, chipping the rock wall next to Connor's head.

Right next to his head.

He ducked in sync with Maya, and together they kept running. He urged her ahead of him, protecting her in case of more bullets.

He'd not heard the gunshot—the guy must have used a silencer.

Had he purposefully missed in order to warn them? Or had Hernandez changed his instructions to his men, wanting them to kill Maya on sight, rather than keeping her alive to be brought to him? Slipping around the corner, he pulled Maya to his other side, out of the line of fire.

So much for hiding in the water, sneaking ashore in the dark. With a glimpse, he took in the surroundings behind the market—a wide-open, grassy field stood between them and another part of town—there wasn't a place to run or hide before Scarface was on them.

Way to go, Jacobson.

Connor braced himself. When Scarface exited the alley to follow them, Connor would pummel him. Pressing himself flat against the wall, Maya, too, he waited for the inevitable. What choice did he have?

Footsteps echoed in the alley, growing closer.

"Connor...no," Maya whispered, her voice choked with tears as she pulled on his arm.

He shrugged her off. There was no time to make her understand.

The guy burst out in the open, and Connor threw himself into him, shoving him into the wall, knocking the breath from his lungs. His weapon clattered across the asphalt, but Scarface quickly recovered and kneed Connor's gut. Pain exploded, radiating through his insides.

Ignore the pain!

The jerk wanted to get free. He wanted his gun.

Connor.

Held.

On.

He couldn't let this guy reach the weapon. Couldn't let him get to the gun.

Connor slammed his fist into the man's face. Hard. Scarface acted dazed. Maybe he'd pass out. Connor scrambled for the gun, but then Scarface was on him and pounded Connor's head into the concrete.

An intense, throbbing ache clawed him from the inside out. Darkness threatened at the edge of his vision. Somewhere in the distance, someone screamed.

Maya? "Run, Maya!"

Gasping for breath, he straightened and gathered his wits. Maya had taken off. Scarface was after her. He'd retrieved the gun, and closed in on her fast.

Connor had to be faster.

She ducked around the corner of a building, music booming inside. The man had almost overtaken her when he disappeared from sight.

Panic flooded Connor—what would he find when he made it to the corner? Would she be gone? Taken again? He focused on saving her, ignoring the voice inside that told him he would always be doomed to fail.

Connor rounded the corner and found himself in another dark alley, empty except for the large crowd gathering up ahead in the street, waiting to get inside a concert. Had Maya taken her chances in the crowd in hopes of hiding?

He merged with the throng, frantically searching for an exotic beauty with long, dark hair. His shorts had dried, so he wasn't any worse for having spent the afternoon snorkeling and looked as though he belonged in the crowd, except his face wasn't in great shape considering the blows he'd taken from Scarface.

"Come on, Maya…" he said under his breath, gritting his teeth. "Show yourself to me."

God, have I lost her? His heart ached with dread as he allowed the throng to move him forward.

Direct my path, Lord. Show me where to find her. Keep her safe…

Across the street a movie theater caught his attention. Through the glass doors he could see people milling about, waiting for the theater to open for seating.

A woman who looked like Maya from the back— similar posture, same hair and clothing—waited in line to enter. Surely, that couldn't be her.

Come on, come on… He willed the woman to turn so that he could see her face.

His line moved forward and the ticket-taker nudged him. "You going in, or what?"

Without taking his eyes from the theater, Connor shook his head and started across the street. He didn't have a ticket to get into the concert anyway. Neither did Maya.

The woman at the theater handed over her ticket and just as she slipped out of Connor's view, he caught a glimpse of her profile.

Maya!

He rushed forward, but reined in his urge to run. He didn't want to draw any attention, especially if Scarface was searching for them.

But if Connor had spotted her, Scarface probably had, too. Connor made his way across the street and as he neared the theater, he realized he would have to pay if he wanted to get inside.

How had she managed? He didn't think she had any cash on her. She'd lost her purse long ago.

Unfortunately, he had to stand in another line, and grew more impatient by the second. Add to that, he wasn't sure which of the three movies Maya would have selected, although the remake of *Romancing the Stone* was more likely than either the slasher or action movie.

A woman in front of him stood at the ticket window now and rifled through her wallet, holding up the line as she searched for money.

Connor stifled a sigh and offered to pay her way along with his. She smiled and thanked him. Had Maya gotten in that way?

He opened the door for the stranger but quickly left her behind as he proffered his ticket to enter the movie.

If Maya wasn't in the theater featuring the romantic comedy, he'd have to slip into the other two movies to find her.

Once inside the darkened room, only the light from the previews illuminated faces. He crept down the aisle, searching, hoping she would be looking for him, as well.

"Maya, where are you?" The question was a whisper under his breath.

Someone who looked like Maya sat a few seats away from the aisle, but she kept her face angled away from him, watching for someone coming in on the other side. Connor excused himself as he aimed for the empty seat next to her. Finally there, he dropped into the seat.

She turned to look at him. "I'm sorry, this seat is saved."

And I hoped you were someone else. Disappointment engulfed him as he made his way over the other seated patrons and out of the row.

Back to his frantic search.

He couldn't live with himself if he let something happen to Maya. Again.

Maybe God hadn't led him in here after all. But he would never give up until he found her.

Saved her.

Always the failure...never the hero.

Connor gritted his teeth, hating the words that dogged him constantly. He had every intention of proving them wrong.

He strolled all the way to the front and stood in the darkest corner. His eyes scanned the faces that filled the theater, illuminated only by the film playing on the screen.

There.

In the far corner of the second row, Maya sat low in her seat.

More patrons had poured in as the time for the movie to start drew near. Connor figured there was one seat left—had Maya saved the last seat for him?

Admiration shot through him—she was in grave danger and yet had the presence of mind to somehow purchase a ticket and hide in a theater full of people, while she waited for Connor to find her.

He searched the faces one more time, making sure he hadn't missed Scarface. The familiar scarred, and now beaten, face wasn't visible in the crowd.

For the moment they had a reprieve.

Slowly, he made his way to where Maya sat, blending into the movie crowd.

His heart breathed a sigh of relief. *Thank You, Lord... for urging me in here.*

He pressed by and stumbled his way over patrons watching the movie. Most were accommodating, but some scowled and made it difficult for him to slip past.

Finally, he sank into the sparely cushioned seat and exhaled. Maya pressed her hand over his and squeezed.

He wrapped his arm around her, wanting to tell her how relieved he was to find her. Instead, he cushioned her head on his shoulder. She leaned toward him and pressed her face into his shirt, her shoulders shaking.

The movie was now in full play. The audio track drowned out her hot sobs against him. He'd give her a few minutes, then they needed to leave. Scarface would find them here soon enough, maybe even with reinforcements.

Connor squeezed his eyes shut, unable to see how they were going to escape the island. Escape this drug lord's long arm. Connor couldn't do this on his own power.

Suddenly the film flickered off, leaving them in complete darkness.

The fire alarm resounded and strobes flashed.

"Fire," someone screamed.

* * *

Maya lifted her head from Connor's chest, her vision blurred with tears.

For a moment, a hush fell over the already quiet moviegoers—no more whispers or eating popcorn or drinking cola.

Milliseconds ticked by. Time stood still.

Then…every person in the theater stood. Screams erupted, including hers, as everyone tried to flee from their prison within the rows. The crowd pushed and shoved toward the exits.

Maya glanced at the ceiling. Why hadn't the sprinklers turned on?

Was her enemy simply trying to flush her out by activating the fire alarm or had he actually started one? Or was this unrelated to her predicament?

Connor dragged her out into the main aisle with him. Although their row was closest to the exit near the screen, Maya wasn't sure they would make it out.

Bodies pressed against her on all sides, threatening to rip her from Connor's grip. They would get trampled if they didn't move with this living, breathing mob.

He held her to him as if she was part of him, rushing forward. She hated the screams accosting her ears. The panic alone could kill if someone fell and people trampled over them.

Too many people, rushing forward. Tugging her. Pulling her away from Connor.

But Maya held tight. This time, she wouldn't let go.

The room grew smaller. The exit no closer.

Smoke bombarded her lungs.

People pressed forward in all directions. Connor practically lifted her off her feet and carried her as he urged others forward, helping them as best he could.

A champion.

Just like she'd thought. Why didn't he see that? He wouldn't trample others, or shove them aside because they were in his way.

Someone had started this fire to get to her. People could die. Because of her.

She and Connor burst through the exit and into the fresh night air, people still pouring out behind him.

"Oh, God, please let everyone make it to safety," she said.

Sirens rang out in the distance, but they would take too long.

Connor gripped her shoulders. "You okay?"

"I'm fine, but we need to do something to help these people."

Frowning, Connor watched the door. Only a few trickled out now, panicked and teary-eyed. "If Scarface started this, he could spot us any minute. Hanging around these people could endanger them even more, but hold on…"

He released his grip on her hand and moved to the exit door that remained ajar, peering inside. He glanced back at her and gestured her over.

"Stand here in the doorway so I can see you," he said.

Maya did as he asked, but didn't like this. "What… what are you doing? You shouldn't go back in there."

Connor disappeared into the darkened, smoky theater. Still no fire sprinklers. Maya peered into the darkness and even between the blinking, flashing lights, she saw nothing.

"Connor!" Panic squeezed her heart. What had he been thinking to go back in there? Several people gathered around her, peering inside.

"Come back. What are you doing?"

The warning lights suddenly stopped, leaving the theater in utter darkness except for the slim light spilling through the door from the lit parking lot.

"Connor?" Maya called his name again, a desperate hopelessness crawling over her.

Suddenly he appeared, stepping from the darkness and holding a little boy not more than five who was wiping his swollen, red eyes.

Maya gasped. "Connor!"

"This little guy was hiding beneath the rows," Connor said.

How did he know to look? Amazed, Maya glanced from Connor to the boy.

He handed the child over to Maya, who took him willingly into her arms. *Poor thing.*

"I think that theater is empty now. I should check the rest."

"No!" Maya was surprised when the other onlookers protested along with her. "No, you've done enough. See? The firemen are here now."

Fire trucks parked in the front near the biggest part of the fire and urged the crowd away from the building.

Assured that Connor wasn't leaving her to endanger himself again, she turned her attention to the boy and examined his face. "Are you hurt anywhere?"

He shook his head. Maya smiled for the boy's sake, but screamed inside. Had his mother or father gone to the restroom, leaving him to watch the movie alone when the alarms kept them from coming back?

In answer to her silent question a woman frantically searched the crowd. "Kevin...Kevin!"

The boy scrambled from Maya's arms and into his mother's. "Oh, my boy." She burst into tears and held him to her.

Connor urged Maya away from the gathering and she followed his gaze.

Scarface...

The man was searching the moviegoers, looking for Maya and Connor. He hadn't spotted them because they were still so close to the doors—Scarface had expected them to bolt as far from the theater as possible. Connor's heroism hadn't just saved Kevin—it had saved them, too.

"Let's get out of here." He gripped her hand and pressed through the people in the streets who'd made it out safely and now watched the flames visible at the front of the theater.

If anyone died because of the fire, because of her, Maya couldn't bear it. There was nothing more they could do now, though. Connor was right. Scarface could hurt more people if they stayed with the crowd.

She ran behind Connor, her legs sluggish, exhausted from swimming and running. She kept up with Connor the best that she could, but it wasn't going to be enough. He drew her around another corner where they both caught their breath away from the crowd and the fire.

"I feel like we're running in circles. Your flight was doomed from the beginning because I was on it. I just can't run anymore. Let me go. Maybe I should call my father again. See if he can get us out of here."

He held her face in his hands and stared at her. "Get a grip. Hang on...just a little longer."

"For what? There is nowhere we can go. Nowhere we can hide."

"We have to keep moving. Have to trust God." Connor grabbed her and urged her to keep walking. "There is a way out, and we will find it if we don't give up."

Her nightmare was coming true.

Running but never getting anywhere. Roberto was somewhere behind her. Somewhere near, calling her name. She could sense him.

A car squealed around a curb and swerved—then drew next to them and stopped before either of them could react. Connor shoved her behind him, protecting her.

What? He was prepared to die for her? She couldn't let him do that, but neither was she getting into that car with Roberto.

The door swung open.

Images flashed in her mind.

She left the Blue Moon Café in Belize. Rushed down the sidewalk. A black car pulled up to the curb.

"Señorita Carpenter, your father." Maya willingly stepped into a vehicle with Roberto Hernandez.

She shook her head, freeing her mind of the images and took off, intending to run this time.

Connor's grip on her arm was too tight.

"Let me go!"

"Maya!" He grabbed her and pressed his face close, his breath fanning her cheeks. "It's Jake. We're getting into this car."

Jake? Relief swept over her, and she crawled into the front seat of an old Chevrolet Impala, sliding to the middle to allow Connor next to her. They'd spent the whole day in such close proximity, she would feel chilled without him next to her, as she'd felt when she'd gone into the theater—surrounded with people, yet without Connor, she was all alone.

Jake sped from the curb and steered down the street, fire trucks and police cruisers passing them on their way to the fire.

"I thought I'd never find you," Jake said. "The island isn't that big, but it's big enough. Thought something happened, especially since I couldn't reach you on your phone. Where have you been?"

"Hiding. All day. What about you? You didn't let anyone follow you, did you?"

Eyes on the road, Jake shook his head. "I laid low at Cheryl's while I tried to get us help or secure a way off the island, just like you said, and waited for your call. When it never came I called you twenty times. Cheryl let me borrow her car a couple hours ago to drive around and look for you. Then I got your message, but I couldn't call you back."

"Why didn't you wait by your phone? Why didn't you answer?" Connor asked.

"I was indisposed, okay? As soon as I got your message I drove down to the marina. Then I saw the fire and I've been cruising around the theater as close as I could get with all the chaos. Was just making my way around the block when I spotted you."

"What about Reg, did you call him?"

"As much as it pained me, yes. I tried." Jake's voice took on an ominous tone. "He's probably working undercover just like we thought. Who knows if he'll be any help or not."

"Did you at least leave him a message letting him know we're in trouble?" Connor asked.

"Of course I did. It was cryptic, at best. What about the local police? Or the Florida Marine Patrol? Can't we trust anyone?"

"No!" Maya and Connor answered simultaneously.

"We know there's at least one cop looking for us and he's working with the drug lord who's after Maya," Connor said.

"So? He might be the only one. There has to be someone we can trust."

Connor exhaled slowly then relayed to Jake everything that had happened.

His brother remained silent for thirty seconds, apparently absorbing everything Connor had told him, but it seemed like an eternity. "And I had hoped you were just out having a good time. That none of our fears would actually come to pass."

"Get a hold of anyone we can rent a plane from and fly out of here?" Connor asked.

"You made it clear we couldn't trust anyone. Who was I supposed to ask?"

"I thought the CBP officer acted suspiciously, so that's probably best," Connor said. "We couldn't have landed in a worse place."

"You mentioned getting a boat. I take it that didn't work out so well," Jake said.

Maya sensed something in his tone—that he had something he was waiting to share.

"I didn't have a chance. Right after I hung up from leaving you a message, Scarface shot at us."

"That's too bad." Jake glanced at Maya, and tossed her a wry grin, but she didn't feel any warmth. "Looks like we're not getting out of here without facing more bullets, except…"

"What are you not telling me, Jake?" Connor asked. "You were supposed to be the one to secure a way out of here. Did you do that or what?"

"If we can't fly then the only way off is the ferry or renting our own boat. Which is what I did."

Connor squeezed Maya's hand. "You rented a boat?"

"Yes. A small yacht, sort of."

"Of course," Connor said. "How'd you do that if we can't trust anyone?"

"Cheryl knows someone and put me in contact. I did some checking and *bingo*."

"And how'd you rent a yacht? How much did that cost?"

"You're worried about cost at a time like this? You'd be surprised how far a little charm will take you."

"Not really. I've seen you in action when it came to a catering van, remember?"

Maya didn't miss Connor's incredulous tone.

"What can I say?" Jake glanced at his brother and almost looked afraid of him. "There's some bad news, though."

"I'm listening." Connor didn't sound happy.

"We have to bring my new friend Candice on the ride."

"I'm not involving another person in this." Maya fairly spewed the words. "Did you tell her how dangerous it was? Do you know if you can even trust her? We could be walking into a trap."

"You're right, except it's not like we have much choice at the moment and I have a good feeling about this, that we can trust her," Jake said.

Connor rolled down the window, letting in some fresh air. "Just get us to your new friend's yacht. Then to Key West—we can drive to Miami from there." Connor turned in his seat to look at Maya and winked. "There's nothing wrong with driving."

Maya warmed under his gaze. She appreciated that

he remembered their previous conversation and tried to inject some humor into a bad situation.

"Hold on. Headlights are coming up on us fast—I'm not sure if they mean to pass us, or if they are going to run us over."

Jake tightened his grip on the steering wheel.

And Maya tightened her grip on Connor's hand.

SIXTEEN

The vehicle behind them closed distance fast. Through the window Connor heard the roar of a modified muffler meant to intimidate.

"Give me your phone," Connor demanded.

Jake tossed the cell in Connor's lap and stepped on the accelerator. "Who're you calling?"

"I'm trying Reg again." Considering Reg's opinion of him, Connor could never have imagined he would be reduced to groveling for his brother's help. That was tantamount to admitting that Reg was right and Connor was a failure.

Maybe he was, after all, but if admitting that was what it took to get help, get them out of this mess, then so be it. He reminded himself of Maya's words regarding life being too short. He was afraid they were about to find out just how short it could be.

The Impala lurched forward as the SUV behind them hit the bumper—hard. Connor pressed his palms against the ceiling of the car. "Get us out of here."

"You think I'm not trying?"

"Lose these guys, head for the marina and for the yacht," Connor said.

Maya clung to his arm, squeezing and cutting into his

flesh with her nails. Jake turned a corner, almost causing them to flip. There wasn't enough traffic for them to lose the SUV on their tail.

Connor couldn't reach Reg, so he tried texting. Maybe Reg couldn't check voice mail, but he could read a text much faster. Under the current driving conditions, Connor struggled with his big fingers.

"Let me have that." Maya took the phone from him. "What are we saying to this brother of yours?"

"Emergency. Assistance required. Use stealth. Golden Key."

He watched Maya expertly type in the words.

"And this is enough information? He'll know what to do?" she asked while she continued to text.

Jake took another quick turn.

"That's short and to the point. If he's any kind of agent, he'll know what to do," Connor said. He was all out of ideas.

That was if Reg wasn't so indisposed in his undercover work that he couldn't come up for air. Then Connor could only hope he would call in someone else to send help—help that could be trusted.

One thing he knew, if they made it out of this, Reg would never let Connor and Jake forget this. *Never.*

Funny how he didn't care that much right now.

Surviving often reduced a person to their most basic needs.

A bullet shattered the back window. Maya screamed and ducked. Again, Connor wished he hadn't left the Glock in the Learjet. That way he could at least return fire.

When they turned another corner, a crowd blocked the street. Jake slammed on his brakes.

"The marina on this side of the island is just one street over. Let's park the car and get lost in the crowd.

Stay with me, but in case we get separated, our boat is the *La Nina*. She's at the far end on the left, in the third slip from the end. Not sure if Candice is already there or not. If not, we'll have to leave without her." Jake blew out a breath. "If that's even possible."

Connor and Maya slid out on one side of the car, and Jake the other, and they hurried into the crowd. Though he and Maya both needed to rest, they ran again, albeit much slower this time. He pulled her behind him, knowing she wouldn't last much longer at this pace, adrenaline or not.

Aware that their pursuers were now on foot, too, Connor pressed through the late-evening partiers and headed to the marina. They would have to jump in and immediately start the boat to escape—he hoped Jake was ahead of them because he'd lost sight of his brother.

The docks in view, they ran across the street and found the specific walkway where Jake directed them. As they ran, wooden planks resounded underfoot and finally, Connor spotted Jake untying the dock lines.

Connor was glad that Jake knew what he was doing when it came to boats. Jake hopped into the small, private yacht just ahead of Connor and Maya.

Just a few. More. Steps…

Connor turned to assist Maya into the yacht and froze.

Scarface held a gun to her temple, his arm around her throat. "Raise your hands so I can make sure that you're unarmed.

"You, too," he said to Jake.

Bile rose in Connor's throat as he did what the man said. His eyes locked with Maya's. *I'm so sorry…*

"You should have let her go it alone. She was all I was after. But now, I need the two of you to join us."

"Us?" Connor asked. How many of these guys would he have to fight in order to escape?

Two more men marched down the length of the dock toward them. Maya was right. They were doomed the instant they took the plane with her on board. Jake climbed out of his friend's yacht to stand next to Connor.

They'd almost made it.

But almost was never good enough.

Connor slowly dropped his hands and lifted one to Maya. The guy must have believed his reinforcements were enough and lowered his weapon from her temple, releasing her to Connor. She ran into his arms and hugged him as if it would be her last.

"I'm so sorry I got you into this," she said, murmuring against his chest.

"You people have caused me a lot of trouble. If I even *think* you're going to try something, one of you will die. Do you understand?"

Jake gave a subtle nod, and Connor squeezed Maya.

"Move," Scarface said, directing the word to her.

"No!" Maya protested.

"Do as he asks," Connor said, releasing her.

The man took a step toward Connor. A fist filled Connor's vision and slammed him in the face. Hard. Blackness winked in and out. Connor swayed and fought to stay conscious. To stay on his feet.

"Payback." The man smirked. "There's more of where that came from after everything you put me through, but first I need you to fly us out of here."

He motioned for his cronies to lead them all away.

They wanted Connor and Jake to fly them out of here? To Colombia?

Roberto's henchman gripped her arm, his fingers pressing into soft flesh, but Maya wouldn't cry out. Nor would she react to his leer.

A ravenous wolf, he ate her alive with his eyes as they roamed down her body. Scarface smacked the man on the head with his gun.

He scowled. "What was that for?"

"Don't get any ideas. Hernandez has something special for her. And I have something special for you if you so much as attempt to act on those impulses."

"And you," he said to the guy who Connor said looked like a bouncer. "You lost her before. Make sure it doesn't happen again, or you'll pay."

Maya had only seen the big man who'd guarded her on the boat from a distance. With a bruise across his face and a bloody, swollen lip, he looked as if, he'd already paid once. He glowered at her now, and she feared what he might do if he had his chance.

Maya eyed Scarface, the man who'd chased her from the beginning. He was protecting her from harm until she was delivered to Roberto. But she shouldn't fool herself into thinking he had a heart. She wondered about how he got his scar. Had Roberto given that to him?

"Now, let's go," he said and grabbed Connor, shoving him forward.

Her captor stood behind her, and forced her ahead with the barrel of his weapon rammed in her back. As one, they hurried along the dock, Jake and Connor treated much the same as Maya.

Legs trembling, she wanted to collapse on the ground, make the men work for it. But she worried that would only end up getting Connor punched again—or worse. These men were beyond cruel.

Her life was nothing—she wanted to lead the men away from Connor and Jake. Why hadn't she done that before? She'd tried to go it alone, but Connor had found her and persuaded her to stick with him. She regretted that decision now, but it was too late to lead Roberto's men away. If she tried, they would hurt Connor and Jake.

Or would they?

Maybe they would chase her. They couldn't return to Colombia without her, and as Scarface already explained, Maya wasn't to be hurt. And if they were running after Maya, that would be a diversion for Connor and Jake—pull the men away from them.

Why make it easy for Roberto or his men?

She hoped that Connor would understand why she had to try—their lives were forfeit as it was. Once they reached Colombia they were as good as dead. All three of them.

In their enemy's hands, torture reigned, and death might not come soon enough.

Maya stopped, and when the man who held her shoved harder, his weapon bruising her, she cried out. He was rewarded with Scarface's attention. "What's going on? I thought I'd already explained myself."

"She's not cooperating. Stopped walking. I shoved her forward. That's all."

Scarface twisted Connor's arm behind his back and forced him to the ground. She'd done this to him. Watching Scarface press Connor into submission like that was more than she could bear and she looked away.

"Let my friends go. I'll cooperate if you'll just let them go," she said, hoping, praying, that he'd listen to reason. "They have nothing to do with this. You don't need them."

He released Connor into the care of his bouncer partner in crime and stepped closer, his face millimeters from hers. "I don't need them?" He ground out the question. "I don't need them? You'd better hope I need them because that's the only thing keeping them alive."

Maya gasped for air.

Near the end of the dock, a police cruiser slowed and red-and-blue lights flashed. Her pulse throbbed against her throat—was it someone coming to save them? Or was it…

The cruiser kept going, taking with it Maya's imagined hopes.

Where was her faith? Why hadn't God answered her prayers? Connor's prayers?

Still in her face, the man smirked. He hadn't even looked at the police car—obviously, it was the officer on Roberto's payroll.

Scarface stepped away from Maya and pressed the muzzle of his gun into Jake's temple. "Now, I want to hear you tell me that I need the pilots. You want them to fly us to our destination. If not, I can dispose of them here and now. Drop them into the water. Nobody will know or care."

Maya had thought Scarface needed them to fly. He'd said as much. But he was cruel and she didn't doubt he would do what he said. Jake stared at her, his eyes a mixture of grief, betrayal and anger.

"You need the pilots. Of course you do." Maya's knees shook. "You can't fly back without them. And you can't hurt them, or they won't be able to pilot the plane."

"That's better." He lowered his weapon.

For a split second, he'd let his guard down. This ordeal had worn on him, as well.

"And you're not supposed to hurt *me*." Maya kicked him hard where it would count.

"Maya, no!" Connor's gut-wrenching shout seemed to come with her action.

Scarface bent over, his face red, veins bulging at his temples. His cronies, the men holding Connor and Jake, held tighter to their weapons and captives. Though still in pain, Scarface slowly lifted his gun and pointed it at Maya's face.

She stood her ground. Better to die here, now, than to be flown back to Colombia. If only Connor and his brother wouldn't have to suffer, as well. Finally, Scarface stood straighter and stared her down.

She took off then, running to the far end of the pier. He ran after her, bullets pelting near her feet.

Men shouted behind her. She couldn't tell if Connor and Jake wanted her to run or to stop. She offered them a diversion. An escape.

Were they fighting their way free?

A weight slammed into her, knocking her into the wooden planks. Scarface was on top of her, pressing her down, his breath ragged in her ear. "You're done causing me trouble." He climbed off and yanked her to her feet in one fluid motion. "Hernandez will have to understand."

His fist flew toward her...

Maya opened her eyes, her head throbbing. Groaning, she reached to her face and gently touched a finger to her eye and cheek, swollen with pain.

Scarface had hit her, that much she remembered.

What happened to drugging her? That was the usual method they'd used to keep her from causing trouble. Regardless, she wasn't sure she felt that much worse with a punch in the face than with the aftereffects of the lingering drugs.

She eyed her surroundings. Buckled in, she sat in a leather seat of a private jet. Then she realized she was not only buckled, but restrained at the wrists by plastic ties that firmly secured her to the seat. Had she made that much of an impression on the men in her attempt to escape?

Glancing around the interior she recognized the plane. Roberto's Learjet. She'd thought it wasn't going to be ready for another week. Had the mechanic lied about that, giving Roberto's men time to catch them? Had he been the one to give them away, calling Roberto?

Shades covered the windows so she couldn't see out, but she could tell they hadn't taken off yet.

Where was Connor? Jake? She squeezed her eyes shut and offered up a prayer, hoping that her stunt hadn't cost them more injuries, or worse—their lives. But then she knew that Scarface needed them.

She turned her head to the side—at least they'd given her that much freedom—and glanced at the window. If only she could see outside. And what if she needed to use the facilities?

Someone sank into the seat across from her. She turned to see Connor's handsome face, and her heart pounded. "Connor…" Emotion choked in her throat. "You're okay. I was so afraid…" She couldn't finish the sentence. "But why aren't you restrained? What's going on?"

Creases carved a deep frown in his rugged features. His eyes roamed over her face, and he reached over and gently touched her cheek. She winced and he pulled away. She would rather he left his hand there—she needed to feel his touch, soak up the reassurance he'd given her so often before.

"What's happening?" she asked again.

"We're prepping for our flight," he said, and kept his eyes locked with hers.

Now she understood. He hadn't been tied up like her because he needed to fly the Learjet. With her restrained, they knew he wouldn't try to run. Scarface would harm her further if Connor didn't do as he was asked.

She could sense that he wanted to tell her something, but couldn't say it—someone else was on the plane. She heard the telltale sounds of an opening refrigerator. Voices kept low somewhere behind them.

He leaned forward and whispered. "Do you trust me?"

When they were snorkeling and in hiding, he'd told her he hoped she would give him a chance to earn her trust, but he'd meant after this crisis was over, or so she'd thought. He didn't know that he'd already earned her trust, and until that moment, neither did she.

She frowned. What did it matter if she trusted him now? But maybe he needed to hear it. Then she realized his simple question instilled a measure of hope in her.

"Yes." She nodded, then added a question of her own. "Are we flying to Colombia?"

Pain sliced through her mind at the words. She'd been through this before. Didn't want to go there again.

He leaned closer then, and she barely heard his next words. "Not if I have anything to do with it."

Abruptly he stood, one of the henchmen urging him away at gunpoint.

A man slipped into the seat across from her, replacing Connor.

Roberto Hernandez!

SEVENTEEN

Connor and Jake taxied the Learjet out of the hangar and onto the runway, preparing for takeoff. Their flight plan had been filed for them, and customs requirements arranged ahead of time. Of course, Connor and Jake would be trusted with none of it—but who had taken care of it? The cockpit unusually quiet, Connor was lost in his morbid thoughts, and guessing by Jake's countenance, his brother was, too.

A sound drew Connor's attention from the control panel, and he turned to see Scarface standing in the doorway.

Blood filled his vision, his thoughts, at the sight of the man. Between Scarface and Hernandez, Connor didn't know which one he wanted to pummel first. Hernandez for his persistence in sending goons after Maya so that he could kill her at a time and place of his choosing.

Or this man.

Acid burned in Connor's gut at the image of Scarface punching Maya, knocking her unconscious. He couldn't stand to think of her tied to her seat, her face bruised.

But this wasn't the right time to lash out. Not yet. He swallowed the burning rage that rose in his throat, and stared at the man, not giving him the benefit of asking what he wanted.

"Hernandez won't tolerate any funny business from you. Try anything, and the woman will pay for it. Do you understand?"

Connor stared. He understood, all right.

When he didn't respond, the swine continued. "All you have to do is deliver us and then you're free to walk away."

The challenge in his smirk told Connor the man knew Connor would never walk away and leave Maya. Told him this man was looking for his chance with Connor. This time Connor nodded, acknowledging what they both knew—they would have another go at each other.

He stepped back into the cabin, and Connor returned his attention to communications with the airport tower and getting the Learjet into the air. Feeling Jake's stare, he glanced at his brother's brooding face.

"Do you think Reg got our message?" Jake asked.

"How would I know?" Connor regretted his harsh tone. "It doesn't matter now anyway."

Jake sighed.

Maybe Connor should have called Reg at the beginning, when he'd first found Maya on the plane. But he hadn't known this would turn lethal within a matter of hours. Just another one of his failures.

"You know we're not leaving Colombia alive, don't you?" Jake asked.

"That won't be an issue unless we land there." Connor didn't watch his brother's reaction. He didn't need to.

As they increased speed, the runway raced beneath them until the Learjet lifted into the air.

"Are you thinking what I'm thinking?" Jake asked, his words barely audible.

"That depends." Connor matched his tone.

"Good one." Jake hesitated. "This is where you're strong, Connor. In the air. This is our chance."

To crash and burn... Did Jake remember Connor's M.O.? Was it really better to die trying? Would Jake agree if Connor voiced the thought?

As the Lear gained altitude, Connor lost himself in the past. All the mistakes he'd made in his life flashed through his mind as if in slow motion. He felt as though he could never get it right. He thought back to the day he'd faced off with Reg. He'd allowed his brother's words to stay with him. To define him.

Always a failure, never the hero.

He'd been desperate to prove his brother wrong. Prove himself wrong. Change his life, his future. Well, no more.

He was out of ideas, all except for one.

There was only One person who could help him—who could save them now. Connor prayed for God to give him inspiration. To help him do something right for once in his life. Regardless of all his failures, Connor believed he'd been created to handle intense and extreme situations.

This was one of them.

"I'll be right back." Connor slid from his seat and ignored Jake's questioning look.

Connor had an idea—a slim chance of an idea. And... it was a risk. Everything needed to be in place or it wouldn't work.

The bouncer filled the door of the cockpit. "Where do you think you're going?"

"The facilities," Connor said. He wasn't going to ask permission and shoved past the man.

"I'll be your escort, so don't try anything."

Connor moved by him and the guy pressed a gun into

his back. Jake's words from what seemed like ages ago resounded in Connor's mind.

"You know what happens when we shoot guns on planes, don't you?"

Connor focused on the galley at the back of the Learjet, and tried to ignore Hernandez and Scarface watching him. In his peripheral vision, he could see that Maya remained secure in her seat. Wrists tied to the armrests. Seat belt buckled tight.

Good.

The way that Hernandez and his men moved about the cabin, Connor knew they hadn't bothered to strap in for takeoff. After all, the luxury jet was built for comfort. Taking normal precautions was inconvenient and bothersome. Connor would use that to his advantage, but it would be dangerous.

In the lavatory, he considered his plan—the risk it involved. He counted the cost to them if it didn't work. After splashing his face with cold water, he stared at his reflection, liquid beads sliding down his exhausted features. Did he have enough clarity to reason this through? Was it the way to go?

Or should he fly them to Colombia, wait for Reg to somehow send them help? But he knew that was a long shot at best.

"God in heaven, help me do the right thing."

He closed his eyes, allowing himself to feel the trauma of his accident again. Remember what it felt like for the earth to come crashing toward him when he experienced engine failure during the test flight of a modified F-22 Raptor—an aircraft that could fly twice the speed of sound.

The investigation hadn't discovered any design, maintenance or system problems, which meant pilot error.

Pilot error!

And the end of his short-lived career at Lockheed Martin as a test pilot.

The reminder along with the cold shock of water to his face sobered him. Maybe Reg was right, but the last thing he needed to think about right now was his brother's words.

Bang. Bang. Bang.

The gun-toting brute standing outside the door wasn't too patient.

"Just a minute." Connor didn't want to make anyone suspicious. Maya would end up paying. He couldn't let that happen again. Had to get her out of this. Failure wasn't an option this time.

He slid the door open and it was Scarface who blocked his path, surprising him. For a split second, he stared Connor down, but Connor didn't flinch. Did the man suspect Connor was planning something?

On the short walk back to the cockpit, the jet hit turbulence and Connor stumbled near Maya, but quickly righted himself.

She averted her gaze and stared out the window, the shade now open for her to see out.

Hernandez watched him over the rim of a glass containing amber-colored liquid. Pain jabbed at Connor's back. What he wouldn't give to turn around and take that gun from Scarface, but for now he had to cooperate. Or pretend to cooperate.

Hang on, Maya. Just hang on.

He struggled to listen to his own words. After everything they'd been through, all their attempts to free themselves from the drug lord's far-reaching power, Connor knew that Maya couldn't get her life back until

Hernandez was routed, one way or another. Neither would Connor or Jake.

More turbulence rocked the plane. *No, no, no*...turbulence would ruin everything.

They would buckle themselves into their seats. His plan wouldn't work. He watched the cabin for signs they were strapping in but saw none.

Maybe they hadn't experienced *real* turbulence. Yet. Connor felt a smile slip into his lips. He hurried forward and dropped into his seat in the cockpit, then glanced at Jake. Scarface stayed in the doorway, watching.

Fine.

He would wait to make his move.

Finally, the man left them alone to fly the plane. Apparently, he'd grown bored with watching the pilots. What could they do anyway without endangering themselves and Maya, too? Connor couldn't help his smirk.

He glanced behind him to make sure they'd been left alone.

Jake looked his way. "Are you thinking to depressurize the cabin? Incapacitate them? All we'd need to do is make sure the passenger oxygen valve is closed. At forty thousand feet they'd be passed out in thirty seconds or less, give or take."

Thirty seconds. Connor stared at the cirrus clouds gathering in the distance above the Gulf of Mexico and shook his head, careful to keep his voice low. "A lot can happen in thirty seconds or less." *Give or take.*

And sometimes thirty seconds wasn't long enough.

Eject! Eject! The words from his accident months ago crowded his thoughts.

Jake gave him a questioning look. *What then?* Connor read in his eyes.

"Snap roll."

Jake released a few colorful words. "Have you forgotten we're in a Learjet? Try that and you'll get us killed. You haven't come up with something better than that? I thought we wanted to survive this."

"Better to die trying…" This time, Connor said the words for Jake to hear.

"I'm sure you've missed Colombia."

From his seat across from her, Roberto Hernandez stared at her, his dark coffee eyes filled with a mixture of satisfaction and conceit.

"How could I? I was only five when…"

Maya lost herself in the black depths of his gaze. A door in her mind flew open—images she'd locked away in a hidden closet poured out. For years, she'd pushed them from her thoughts, clawed her way out of the terror and dread.

But Roberto's eyes—eyes she hadn't looked into for twenty-three years—had unlocked the door, breaking through her barricade. There was nothing she could do to stop the flood of memories.

Sunshine warmed her face on the playground. She laughed, her hair flying back as she swung high. She jumped from the swing.

Her beautiful mama sat on the bench talking to her friend, Paquita.

Maya's feet hit the ground. She took off running but her hair caught on something. No. Wait. Someone held on to her by the hair, pulling her back.

A scream erupted, but was stifled by a hand covering her mouth. Strong arms wrapped around her.

Mama grew smaller in the distance. The man carried her the wrong way. Maya screamed. But Mama didn't hear. Finally, Mama looked up, her eyes searching the playground.

And then, her eyes locked with Maya's even from this far away. Her face scrunched up and she screamed and ran toward Maya. But the man stuffed Maya in a van. He pressed tape over her mouth and forced a bag over her head.

The van sped from the curb and rushed through traffic. Though Maya was strapped into a seat, the force of the turns threw her this way and that. She cried. She didn't understand what was happening. She wanted her mama. Her papá.

Maya couldn't remember when she fell asleep or how she ended up in the dark, small room. She could barely see. The air was too stuffy. The room too small. She cried, screamed and kicked on the door until finally she gave up and curled in a ball on the hard mattress that was thrown on the floor.

A woman Maya had never met entered into the room to bring her food three times a day and allow her to use the facilities. Maya begged to be allowed to see her mama or her papá. But the woman only frowned and told her to be quiet.

Maya got sick. She shivered. The woman brought her a blanket and made her drink a lot of water. Then Maya was hot and sweaty. More shivers, more sweat. The woman looked worried.

Maya wasn't hungry anymore. She lost her appetite. The room was so dark and small. She only wanted to be free to run again. To play again. One day the woman came into her room and brought Maya to sit in a room with a man.

She sat in a large, spacious area with beautiful rugs and paintings and waited while the man stared at her with the same dark eyes that stared at her now. But he was a much younger Roberto then. Maya clung to the woman's dress because the awful man scared her.

And he scared her now...

Maya squeezed her eyes shut and looked away. And remembered the rest...

The woman took her back to her dark room. That night she came for Maya and sneaked her away to her papá. He kissed Maya and said goodbye and sent her on an airplane with Mama.

The woman had risked her life, Maya was certain. Roberto had probably killed her himself. If not for her, Maya would have died instead. She couldn't have escaped of her own accord, just as she couldn't escape now.

"You've grown into such a lovely young woman, Maya. I wish things could be different." He leaned forward and put a hand on her knee.

Maya shuddered. There was no woman to help her escape today. There was only Connor, and even her champion hadn't been able to free her from Roberto's clutches. No. There was only Maya. And just as she'd done for more than twenty years, and with God's help, she would take control of her life back and save herself, save them all, from this man.

A plane had taken her to freedom that day years ago. And a plane would send her back to meet her death. Unless she did something.

At her reaction, Roberto simply laughed. He enjoyed toying with her and the last thing she wanted to do was give the man satisfaction. But he had the upper hand now. What could she do to take him down? Especially tied up like this.

"Do you know why I took you that day?"

Maya said nothing, though her father had told her.

The truth of that had almost undone her. She didn't want to hear it again from Roberto's lips.

He continued, apparently not caring if she responded. She cut her gaze back to him. By the look on his face, Maya could tell he was thinking back, remembering the past, as Maya had just done.

"He took my son. Your father took my son from me." Roberto moved into the seat next to her.

He ran a finger down her arm, making her skin crawl. "You think I'm a bad man. But your beloved father is a murderer." He spat the words. "I vowed to repay him. Now I have my chance. Though I lost you before, I won't lose you again."

Maya turned to face her abductor. "Are you going to kill me, then, after so many years?"

"I can't break my vow, can I?" The cold, heartless tone of his words cut her heart open, and poured an icy chill inside.

"So why don't you get it over with?" she asked.

"All in good time… I want to savor this moment. The look of fear in your eyes."

Maya struggled to breathe under his weighty gaze. *Take control of your life back.*

"Are your men really that threatened by me that I have to be tied up? I need to use the facilities."

Roberto laughed and nodded at one of his cronies.

How Maya loathed his laugh. She hoped and prayed for a chance to be free from him forever, but what would that take? His death? No. There had to be another way. Even if given a chance, she could never kill another human being.

Except that my father's blood runs in my veins. The simple thought—born of years of fear and dread—tore at her insides.

The bouncer approached her and pulled a knife, angling it so Maya could see the sharp edges glisten. Her heart battered against her chest. Did Roberto mean to kill her like this? Here and now?

His brute grinned then reached for the plastic ties securing her wrists to the armrests. But he never made it.

The plane took a sudden dive. Roberto and his henchman floated to the ceiling. Terrified shrieks filled the cabin.

Maya's stomach flew into her throat. She wouldn't die at Roberto's hands… She would die in a plane crash.

EIGHTEEN

"What makes you think this will work?" Jake yelled at him now, a sharp contrast from their shared whispers earlier. "You don't know if it'll hurt them. You can't know."

A string of profanity resounded from the fuselage, accompanied by screams and yells. If this didn't work, Connor didn't want to think about what Hernandez would do.

"I have to try," Connor said. An abrupt negative G had sent Roberto and his men to the ceiling, but that was only half of what Connor planned. "Besides, it ain't over yet."

Jake glanced at Connor, his frown spreading into a grin.

The Learjet screamed toward the earth in an arc.

"Brace yourself," Connor said, though he knew his brother understood what would happen next. "If this doesn't work, and I'm in trouble back there, then you have no choice but to roll."

"No." Jake shook his head. "I can't…"

"You *can*. The plane won't come out of it unscathed, but maybe we can survive. If you don't, then all our lives are forfeit."

A bead of sweat slid down Jake's temple. "How will I know?"

"You'll know."

The higher the speed, the higher the Gs. The more abrupt the pull, the more punishing the force—and Connor counted on that force to press him into his seat.

He counted on that same force to yank Roberto and his men from the ceiling and slam them into the floor. Hard enough and it might knock them out. As a fighter pilot, Connor was trained to resist the G-force effects on his body so he wouldn't lose consciousness, but he couldn't risk taking things that far.

He pulled back abrupt and hard on the control yoke, cringing at the sound of bodies hitting the fuselage, and prayed for Maya's safety.

Hang on, Maya, just hang on.

Then…besides the screams of the jet engines, silence was the only sound that met his ears from the cabin.

Were Hernandez and his men truly incapacitated?

Seconds…I have seconds…

Leveling out, he released his restraints, grabbed the Glock from under the seat and exited the cockpit into the cabin.

A familiar stench slammed into him—someone had gotten sick.

Maya stared at him wide-eyed and pale.

Hernandez moaned on the floor.

Another man lay motionless, a knife in his chest. The other two were sprawled at the back of the cabin.

With quick precision, Connor cut the plastic ties from Maya's wrist and then her ankles, remembering the moment he'd done the same thing barely two days ago.

Holding his Glock at the ready, he glanced at Maya. "Are you all right?"

"Yes," she said. She unbuckled her seat belt and stood, understanding the urgency in gaining control of the plane.

One of the men's guns lay on the floor and Connor picked it up. After chambering a round, he handed it to Maya. "Watch Hernandez."

Maya aimed the weapon at the drug lord, her hand trembling at first. Connor slid his hand under hers to steady her aim. "Can you do this?"

She nodded, never taking her eyes from the man who'd abducted her. Who wanted her dead.

Connor headed to the back of the cabin to secure the other two. Scarface rose to meet Connor with a weapon of his own, but Connor was quicker and rammed into him.

A gunfight was the last thing he wanted. Stray bullets could injure Maya or Jake or potentially depressurize the cabin. He wrestled the man, pounding his wrist against the wall so he would release his gun. Pain squeezed his head when Scarface knocked him into the refrigerator. Connor returned the favor, ignoring the throbbing in his skull.

Ignoring the fear that this man would best him.

Then he couldn't save Maya. She and Jake would die because of his failure.

But then Connor remembered something… He allowed the images to accost him again.

Back on the dock, the man had toppled on Maya, preventing her escape. He'd lifted her to her feet then slammed his fist into her face. Rage burned Connor's thoughts. Colored his actions.

That was all he needed.

He stood now, facing Scarface, locking eyes with

him. The familiar smirk slid into the man's lips. He lifted his hand and beckoned Connor toward him.

"I know you want to kill me for what I did to your woman," he said, smiling. "But that's not going to happen. You've already tried repeatedly to save her and failed. When it's all over she's going to suffer even more. I'm looking forward to it."

Connor bristled at the words, at the intimidation tactics. He wanted to shove them far away, pay no attention. If only he didn't fear they were true.

You tried to save her and failed...

"Come on, then." He beckoned Connor forward again. "You're afraid to die, aren't you?"

Behind the man, Maya turned her head to look at Connor. The bruise and swelling on her beautiful face knifed through him again. His gaze flicked back to the man who taunted him, wanting the fight.

A strap hung from a storage cabinet mere inches from the man's head, giving Connor an idea.

"No. I'm not afraid to die. But you should be," Connor said and shoved him against the wall. Before Scarface could react, stopping him, Connor wrapped the strap around his neck, pulling tighter and cutting off his oxygen. "Because if you killed me, then who would fly the plane?"

"Hernandez," Scarface squeaked out, tugging against the strap on his neck.

Connor eased up. "Hernandez what?"

"He's a pilot."

Hernandez was a pilot? That explained who'd filed the flight plans, and it also made either Connor or Jake dispensable, but not both of them. Hernandez needed at least one of them to fly with him. The Learjet required two pilots. He'd brought them both along to use one of them as a negotiating tool if needed. Plus, he appeared to enjoy spending his time taunting Maya, rather than flying the Learjet.

Tugging hard, Connor released the strap when the man lost consciousness. He quickly tied Scarface's wrists, knowing he'd come around too soon. Then Connor looked Maya's direction.

Hernandez was getting to his feet, and Maya aimed her weapon at him. The bouncer had been unconscious at the back of the plane but was stirring now, as well. Funny, he was the guy Connor expected his maneuver would affect least.

Maybe there was truth in the old adage "the bigger they are, the harder they fall."

Whatever. The next few seconds would be win or lose as Connor went to restrain him.

Roberto gripped the armrest and got to his knees. Then he stood to his feet and straightened to his full height, his expression livid. Before he looked at her, he appeared to regain his composure as though he believed he still maintained control over the situation. Over Maya.

But he was wrong. She was in control now.

Still, when he looked at her, his dark eyes flashed, sending terror twisting through her core.

Maya's knees shook, her hand trembled. Why? She had the gun now. Connor had given it to her to protect herself. She aimed the weapon now, but she'd never fired a gun before. Never hurt anyone or anything.

Protect yourself.

She fingered the trigger.

Roberto stood inches from her now. His tall form mocked her, intimidating her. His eyes laughed at her.

He took a step forward. "You can't kill me, Maya,"

he said, his eyes bearing the same conceit she'd seen before. "You've grown up living a soft, protected life."

And what was wrong with that? But she said nothing in the face of the anger and bitterness rising in her chest. Did she dare engage this man in conversation? No, she had no words for him.

Maya stepped back. They were dancing their last dance—a terrible, sick dance.

Roberto took another step. "And if you somehow escape me now, there is nowhere you can go to be safe. I will always hunt you. And as you already know, I will always find you no matter how long it takes."

And Maya stepped back, but this time the seat blocked her path. She was trapped. She couldn't go any farther. Roberto drew closer until the gun's muzzle pressed against his broad chest.

He laughed again. "You're no murderer, Maya."

He was right, she wasn't.

"You forget…" Her voice croaked, barely a whisper. "My father's blood runs in my veins."

Roberto's eyes narrowed, but in them she saw fear. *Fear!*

"I don't want you dead, but I *will* protect myself." The gun shook violently in her hand now. She didn't want to kill this man, but how else would this ever end? How else could she get her life back? But would she really be able to pick up her old life as if nothing had happened after killing a man?

If this ended in her killing Roberto she would know for certain she was the daughter of Eduardo Ramirez— her father in Colombia. God was not her father at all.

No. That was wrong. Connor's words resonated through her mind. She had a new father now. A Father in Heaven. She was a new creation.

In an instant, Roberto moved to take the gun from her. They wrestled. She struggled to hold on to the weapon, to squeeze the trigger.

Suddenly, Connor appeared in the midst of the thrashing, but Roberto wouldn't let go of her or his grip on the gun. Neither would she.

A shot ran out, thunderous and earsplitting.

Two more deafening shots pierced her ears.

Connor froze. Roberto stared at her. She'd shot him, hadn't she?

She released the weapon to Roberto and Connor, who wrestled for it, their arms stretched, pointing the gun up and away. The gun went off again, and Maya covered her aching ears, afraid she would be rendered deaf, if she wasn't shot dead first.

A warning went off somewhere.

Oxygen masks dropped as the engines screamed and the jet took a dive, descending rapidly. All of it happened in the same split second of time.

Blood spilled across Roberto's shirt, and his eyes glazed over and rolled back in his head. He fell to the floor.

"Strap in." Connor gripped and shook her out of her shock, speaking above the din. "Put on the mask and quick."

Connor grabbed his jacket from an overhead bin, for some reason, and rushed to the cockpit, leaving Maya alone. She buckled in and secured the oxygen mask, but sucking in the air did nothing to calm her. Breathing did nothing to help her pounding heart.

Her pulse raged in her ears. Had she shot Roberto? Was he dead now?

She squeezed her eyes, tears streaming from the corners. She wasn't sure what happened. But what did that matter now? They were going to crash. She was going to die anyway.

Oh, God in heaven, forgive me if I shot Roberto. If I killed him, forgive me. And if you see fit, don't let it end this way. Please...oh, God...don't let us die.

Maya shut her eyes, praying hard. Images flashed against her lids—her entire life passing before her in mere seconds...the last seconds of her life.

Her father's face appeared in her mind as she remembered it over twenty years ago. Smiling at her. Swinging her around. Laughing with her. Loving her. *Oh,* Papá...

And now, she would die before he did, all because of the crimes of his past. She would never see him again unless they met on the other side. Thinking about him in a positive way always ended with what he'd done to her.

Maya knew she couldn't die still holding on to that burden. She knew what she had to do.

Lord, I forgive my father for his actions. Actions that stole my family, my life, from me.

I forgive.

How much time did she have? Seconds? Images of Connor holding her, kissing her, played across her mind.

She smiled, embracing the warmth that enveloped her in the face of her approaching demise.

NINETEEN

Once in his seat in the cockpit, Connor pulled his own oxygen mask in place then drew in a deep breath, ignoring the ache pounding through his body. He had to see this through, to finish this. He couldn't fail this time.

Jake's eyes grew wide behind his mask, but Connor could still see the relief in his face. "You look like you're glad to see me," Connor said through the microphone on the mask.

Jake nodded. "Are we in control?"

"We're in control."

"What did I tell you about guns? The pressurization system is struggling with a slow decompression. When the warning light came on, I went ahead and dropped the masks. If nothing else, I thought I should make a rapid descent to 10,000 just to shake things up for you back there."

"Thanks." Connor chuckled.

"We're good on fuel," Jake added.

If fuel was a concern, they'd need to fly higher and use the oxygen longer, possibly using up their limited supply.

"Good thing we're not flying over a mountain range

right now," Connor said. They'd have to fly at an altitude in which they couldn't survive without cabin pressure.

"Is that your attempt at injecting a positive spin on this?"

"You're onto me." Connor grinned, but he could tell that Jake wasn't ready to count their blessings yet.

Still, his brother had everything under control without him. Connor sighed, releasing the pent-up tension of the past few minutes. Make that the past few days.

"I contacted Miami," Jake added. "We're going for an emergency landing there. I'm not taking any chances landing on an island again where this drug lord could have people working for him. But I couldn't exactly tell Miami what happened back there. Just told them we lost pressure."

"They'll have a hard time working for a dead man," Connor said.

Jake's silence told Connor that he waited for an explanation, but Connor was still trying to wrap his mind around everything.

"I thought I'd lost you back there," Jake said. "What happened?"

The Learjet reached the lower altitude and cabin pressure stabilized. Connor ripped off his mask, as did Jake.

"You thought something happened to me? I told you to roll. Why didn't you do what I asked?"

"You told me I would *know*." Jake tossed Connor his familiar, accusing glare. "Well, I never knew. There wasn't a signal or anything. I wasn't going to risk our lives unless I knew for sure it was necessary. And apparently, it wasn't."

There was a smile behind Jake's scowl now. Connor laughed and reached over to squeeze his shoulder. "You did good, bro. You did good."

"*I* did good? You're the one who saved us. So, what happened back there? Are you going to spill?"

"Half of the bad guys are dead."

"Only half?" Jake's laugh was incredulous. "What about the others? They going to cause us problems?"

Connor sighed. "No, I don't think so. Besides Hernandez, another guy had an accident with a knife. Must have occurred during my maneuver. Two of the living are tied up in the back of the plane."

"And Maya? She okay?" Jake asked.

"I'm not sure she'll ever be okay." *Not after this.* Connor hated hearing the spoken truth, to even think about it. "I'm going to check on the bad guys and Maya. You contact Miami again and apprise them of our full passenger manifesto, the good, the bad and the ugly. This time, we want law enforcement to meet us there."

Connor looked his brother in the eyes. An understanding passed between them—neither of them knew how this whole thing would affect their lives, but it wasn't as if it would go away quickly. Connor was more worried about how this would affect Jake's current job as a commercial pilot. Hopefully there wouldn't be a fallout because he'd done nothing wrong, but that didn't always matter.

He shoved from his seat, exited the cockpit and entered the cabin, his first thought and concern for Maya. She'd removed her mask, her beautiful almond eyes redrimmed.

Pulling his gaze from hers long enough to take in the resulting disarray, he could see his two captives remained unconscious, secured with straps.

Maya's abductor, a murderer who had relentlessly hunted her down, was dead, and Connor hoped her worries were over. That she could get her life back. But there was still the matter of the authorities learning her identity as the daughter of a wanted drug lord. There was no way around that now. Surely, her fears that they would use her to get to her father were unfounded.

Offering a pensive smile, he dropped into the seat across from her and leaned forward, unsure what she needed from him. He eyed her closely, trying to read her mood. What she was thinking.

"It's all over, Maya."

Her lips trembled and she looked out the window. Connor wished he had a better track record with women, more experience. He couldn't think of anything he wanted to do more than hold her and reassure her as he'd already done so many times before. But now they were free from the situation that had shoved their lives together.

Weren't they?

And suddenly he didn't know what to do. What she wanted.

Maya's gaze drifted back to him. The pain he saw there shook his soul, but he caught something else, something that simmered just below the surface. Something he'd seen before.

She *needed* him.

Inside him, a question that he didn't want to ask burned. Once there was distance from this situation, distance from each other, would they still feel the same way?

Looking into her eyes now, Connor knew what he wanted with her, and he knew what he was willing to give up in order to make that happen. He just didn't know where she stood. But he did know that he would have to be patient. He shoved aside the thoughts because he had some news to deliver, and she probably wasn't going to like it.

"We're headed to Miami now. The police—FBI, ICE, DEA—I have no idea who else will probably meet us there. No getting out of that. Just thought you should prepare yourself."

She nodded.

"I know you're afraid that they will use you to get to your father. Let's hope you're wrong, Maya. Let's pray that you can get your life back, okay?"

Again she nodded. Connor prayed for their safe landing and that the right people would meet them. Silently, he prayed for God's direction regarding any future with Maya.

After this, neither of them would ever be the same.

Connor was forever changed because he'd lost his heart to Maya—the Colombian drug lord's daughter. Since the first time he'd met her on this Learjet, everything between them had changed.

Everything.

Was there anything there for him? Did she care for him? After all this was over, did he dare hope for a chance with her?

"Maya…" he whispered, but before he could continue, Jake's voice interrupted.

"Connor, I need you. We're heading into the landing sequence, and there's smoke in the cockpit."

What now? Connor frowned. He wouldn't have time to say everything he wanted and needed to say.

"Go. You're not done saving us yet."

Her words meant the world to him; she counted on him. Was she putting too much hope, too much trust, in him?

For the first time in a long time, Connor shoved his doubts away.

* * *

Maya put her trust in God and in the pilot he'd brought into her life. She'd feared trusting anyone for so long, but how could she have any doubts about Connor? He was the most reliable, dependable person she'd ever met.

He could have left her to face this alone from the beginning. Could have turned her over to the authorities in Golden Key, which would have ended in disaster for her, but he'd done none of those things.

He hadn't let her down yet.

But none of the misgivings that snaked through her had a thing to do with him and everything to do with her. She struggled with her past despite that the source of her worst nightmares was dead. In truth, it was *because* Roberto was dead that she struggled.

For the most part, Roberto and his men could no longer cause her harm, whether dead or alive. She owed Connor for that.

But he hadn't saved her completely—she'd killed Roberto herself. The simple fact left her in a state of shock. She'd taken another human being's life. It didn't matter that he was a drug dealer and a murderer.

Surviving on next to no sleep, she rubbed her eyes and reminded herself that she wasn't thinking straight. Tomorrow this would all look differently. She'd remember that the man would have killed her. She'd done what she had to do to defend herself.

As she stared out the window, her thoughts a jumble, the jet hit turbulence on the approach to Miami. Maya squeezed the armrest, hoping that Connor and his brother had figured out why smoke had filled the cockpit. She hoped, maybe beyond hope, that the smoke wouldn't affect their safe landing.

Facing death, she realized how much she wanted to live. A chance to find out if she had anything with Connor. If they landed she would get that. Maybe. Away from the pressure cooker of the past few days, would they decide they were too different? If so, then stepping off the plane and facing the authorities, explaining everything to them, would magnify those differences.

An upstanding citizen like Connor with a good family heritage didn't have any business connecting with a woman like Maya.

Looking out the window, she watched the earth draw closer. The ocean filled her view, sprinkled with small, tropical islands here and there—a stark reminder of their recent ordeal.

The city loomed in the distance until finally, the airport runway grew closer, palm trees and buildings sped by. The plane touched down and bounced, once, twice, then remained connected with the runway. Maya released the breath she'd held as she prayed silently.

From her window, she could see the fire trucks and other emergency and law-enforcement vehicles headed in the Learjet's direction.

Roberto Hernandez's Learjet.

Maya sucked in a breath and tried to calm her racing heart. The authorities would want answers. They would want to know everything.

Connor stood next to her, leaning over her seat. "Maya," he said.

She looked up at him and realized he'd been trying to get her attention. Fear had kept her eyes glued to the mayhem outside.

"We have to exit the plane now."

She nodded and stood, then stumbled back. He steadied her. "It's going to be all right. Just tell the truth."

"I have lived in this country almost my entire life and they have never known that I was Eduardo Ramirez's daughter. Connor, he's wanted in ten countries." Her legs shook. "I went to meet him—a wanted man."

Connor ushered her forward and whispered in her ear from behind. "I'm here to face everything with you."

His words held a measure of reassurance as did his touch, but when the pressure was on, he would change his mind. Eric dropped into her thoughts again—he'd left her as soon as he'd learned the truth. Connor just didn't understand how difficult, how ugly, life would be now. Maya had to admit that she wasn't sure, either.

Jake's chest rose as he drew in a breath. "You ready?" he asked.

Connor pressed his lips into a flat line, then gestured for Jake to open the door. Bright sunlight spilled into the cabin. He took the first steps outside. Connor squeezed her arm. His smile was plastered on for her benefit, but in his eyes she knew he was concerned about their reception, as well. None of them really knew how their story would be received.

After Jake, it was Maya's turn to step outside. She took the first step, and then the next and finally her foot pressed onto the pavement. Connor drew up behind her and urged her away from the Learjet. Several fire trucks were parked around the jet and firemen searched for any trouble. Just like before on the island, only this time, there was nothing to fear from Roberto.

She allowed Connor to hurry her to a safe distance where emergency personnel gathered around them, wanting to make sure no one was injured. She listened as if from the far end of a tunnel while Connor explained about the men on the plane—that two were deceased and two were dangerous but were in need of medical attention.

The whole thing was surreal. But Connor never released her, holding her close to him with his left arm. Questions were asked and minutes went by until finally she saw two bodies being carted off the Learjet.

Two more were escorted off by law enforcement, their hands cuffed behind their backs. Maya wondered why she and the pilots weren't treated the same—for all these men knew, they were the guilty parties.

A man rushed toward Jake and Connor and then embraced Jake, long and hard. Like good friends. Or brothers. The man—an older version of Jake and Connor—looked at Connor and hesitated. Maya read him well—he wanted to hug his brother, but wasn't sure his brotherly affection would be welcome.

She sensed that Connor's brother regretted his words and wanted to resolve their issues.

Finally, the man grabbed Connor and hugged him regardless of permission. Though Maya didn't understand the pained expression on Connor's face, she smiled, instantly liking his brother. When Connor stepped away, he turned his attention to her and smiled. In that smile, she could almost believe that things were going to work out, but there was something else he was hiding.

"Maya, this is my brother, Special Agent Reg Jacobson." Connor pressed his hand against her elbow.

She thrust her hand out. "Nice to meet you. I'm Maya Carpenter."

Though the agent took her hand and shook it, his eyes subtly narrowed.

"How did you know to meet us here?" Connor asked Reg.

"After all those messages you left me? It didn't take

me long to learn you were headed to Miami for an emergency landing. I have connections, or did you forget?" His easy smile for Connor shifted when he turned his gaze back to Maya.

He studied her a little longer than she would have liked. What did he know about her? Did he think she had corrupted his brothers? That she was to blame for their involvement? In a way he would be right.

TWENTY

Over his brother's shoulder, Connor could see the intimidating-looking men approaching their cozy little circle. DEA or ICE looking for answers, he was sure. He felt the beads of sweat growing on his forehead, but it had nothing to do with the men.

"Give me a minute," he said to Reg. The pain in his side, though intense, had grown numb. At the same time he felt himself growing weaker. He'd needed to help Jake land, and now he had to talk to Maya. Thank goodness she couldn't see the blood he knew had to be visible under his jacket.

Reg's eyes cut to Maya then back to Connor, his gaze probing. Connor knew his brother well enough— he could tell that Reg recognized that something was wrong, but he nodded his agreement and stepped over to talk to Jake. Connor was grateful.

He hadn't expected the reception he'd received from Reg. It caught him off guard. But he would worry about that later. For now he tugged Maya a little ways from Reg and Jake and the throng of emergency and law-enforcement personnel. Expectant, she looked up at him.

He was still a little stunned from everything. He gripped her shoulders. There was so much he wanted to say to her, so much he'd wanted to say before they'd landed but circumstances had prevented him. He hadn't had the time to tell her what he was feeling, and he wasn't going to get the time now.

There was only one way he knew to make her understand, and he wasn't sure even that would work. "Maya," he whispered.

He searched her eyes, looking for something that told him what he wanted to know. His gaze roamed her beautiful face, smooth complexion and perfect nose then paused at her heart-shaped lips. Lips that he'd watched tremble and frown too many times.

Drawing closer to her, he knew what to do and held out his hand. "Come here," he said.

She pressed her palm into his and stepped into his embrace. When she pressed her face into his shoulder, he could feel the heat of her breath, the warmth of her body, through his shirt where his jacket opened. He swept his hand down her back and the length of her hair. He wanted so much more with this woman, but they had each been through a lot in the past few hours. Asking for more now would be too much.

He lifted her chin and, taking courage from the fact that she didn't step back, Connor pressed his lips fully against hers. He'd wanted to kiss her so she would know that he wanted her in his life.

At first, he could tell she held back, and his heart stumbled, fearing he'd lost her before he'd even had her. Then she slid her arms over his chest and around the back of his neck, pulling him down and closer, her fingers playing with his hair.

Amazing sensations swam through his insides and coursed through every part of him as he wrapped his arms around her. His head was lost in the essence of all that was Maya. His heart was all he had left and he deepened the kiss, pouring all of his heart into it.

"Connor…" Maya whispered his name against his lips. "We shouldn't do this. You shouldn't be seen fraternizing with me. That could get you into more trouble."

He didn't want to let her go but now was the time for words, and saying those words would be the riskiest thing he'd ever done—laying his heart out there. "I know we got off to a rocky start, but I want you in my life. I'm falling in love with you."

She pressed her fingers against his lips. "Shh…"

Her eyes brimmed with tears. Who would have thought tears could cut a man's heart like that? "We're too different. It would never work," she said.

He saw in her eyes what he'd wanted to see—a chance at love. Why was she telling him it wouldn't work? Then he knew. "This is because of your father, isn't it?"

Maya took that step away, but Connor squeezed her arms and pulled her back to him, pressing his face near hers. How did he make her understand? "I don't care about your father, Maya. I'm not like Eric."

"You were wrong about me. I *am* my father's daughter—I *killed* Roberto. I *killed* a man."

"No, Maya, no." Connor shook his head, so relieved at the truth. "You didn't kill Roberto. That credit belongs to me."

Her eyebrows squeezed together, her expression stunned. "Wh…what? No, that's not possible."

"It *is* possible. Roberto got off a few shots from the gun I gave you, but I shot him with the Glock. Now, what you have to decide is if you can live with *me* because I killed a man."

"But you were protecting me," she said, color quickly

returning to her face along with the tiniest hint of a smile.

"As you would have protected yourself, had you been the one to shoot him." But Connor understood that if Maya had killed Roberto, it would have haunted her forever. She struggled to let go of the fact her father was a Colombian drug lord. "Who your father is doesn't define who you are, Maya."

Connor sensed that Maya still wasn't convinced and desperation filled his soul. He tugged her to him again and hugged her, never wanting to let go. He thought of his ex-fiancée, Darrah, and how he'd put his wants and needs above hers. He wouldn't let that happen again if Maya would just give him the chance.

"Connor." Maya spoke softly into his ear.

He eased from the hug and looked at her. She kissed him this time, desperately. But he knew, he *knew,* that she believed it would be their last.

Someone cleared a throat, and Connor ended the kiss.

DEA agents stood around them. An agent stepped forward. "Maya Carpenter?"

She nodded. "Yes."

"If you'll follow me, please, we have a few questions for you."

"Remember what I told you." Maya hugged him again and stood on her toes to whisper into his ear. "They will use me to get to my father. I can't let my life destroy yours," she said.

God, let her be wrong about this. Dizziness swept over him.

"Connor?" Maya asked. She pulled her hands away— they were covered in blood. His blood.

He hadn't realized she'd thrust her hands beneath his jacket.

"You're bleeding!"

People around him swayed and tilted. Maya screamed. She reached for him, but they were taking her away from him. Connor tried to reach out, to keep her with him, but his arms wouldn't respond, nor would his legs carry him. Reg's faced filled his vision.

"You're a real hero, Connor. I never doubted that, despite what I said. I'm sorry about everything."

Connor was on a gurney now, being wheeled into an ambulance. He grabbed Reg's arm, effectively keeping the gurney from going anywhere. At least he'd been able to muster that much strength. "I need a favor."

His brother arched a brow. "This doesn't have anything to do with Maya Carpenter, daughter of Colombian drug lord Eduardo Ramirez, does it?"

"How did you guess?" Connor managed a little sarcasm.

Reg leaned in and spoke in a low tone. "You don't want to get involved with her."

Squeezing Reg's arm a little too tightly, Connor tugged him closer. "I'm already involved. Now see to her. Make sure she's all right. That she knows I want her in my life."

"You're not thinking straight. We'll talk about this when you recover."

The gurney shoved forward and into the ambulance despite Connor's protest. Where was Jake? He would understand. But Connor couldn't fight the darkness threatening anymore and shut his eyes, leaving the outcome in God's hands.

Lying in the hospital bed, Connor thought about how no matter what he did, it seemed as though he always ended up in the hospital, recovering from his injuries.

After being processed by the authorities, the Learjet would be released to Connor to complete his transaction. A few repairs were in order, including the problems causing the depressurization and the smoke in the cabin, but then Connor would return the jet to Troy in Virginia and receive the rest of his money.

As for him, the wounds he'd experienced this go-round were for a far different reason from his last hospital visit and not because he'd crashed a costly airplane. Nor would mending from a bullet in the side take much time at all. He'd had to stay an extra night because of his blood loss, but he would be released tomorrow morning.

His other injury—the one to his heart—would take far longer to mend, if it ever did. He feared he'd lost Maya, and would never get that chance with her.

Unfortunately, the hospital setting served as a constant reminder of his months-long recovery from his test-pilot crash, when Darrah had broken off their engagement, declaring she couldn't live with the constant fear.

Funny that here he was again, worried about his relationship with a woman.

Jake, Reg and their mother had spent time with him over the past several hours, and he'd answered a kazillion questions from various law-enforcement entities, but no Maya. Nor would Reg give him any details as to her whereabouts or what was happening. Jake didn't know anything, nothing new there. Besides that, Connor hadn't exactly been in a talkative mood.

Maya had made it clear that things wouldn't work out between them. Connor hadn't believed her, but regardless of what he believed, he had to consider the possibility that she didn't want to be contacted or found by him. To pursue her when she didn't want to be pursued would make him a stalker.

Not as though he could do much from a hospital bed, though, except email. That wasn't working so well anyway.

Every time he typed up a long email to send through her business website, he ended up deleting it. He couldn't tell her everything without knowing how she felt. What she wanted from him, if anything.

He would give her plenty of time, though, and maybe she would make first contact. Considering his last words, proclaiming that he was falling in love with her, the next move was hers.

Rubbing his scruffy jaw, he leaned his head back against the pillow and closed his eyes. He was at a crossroads regarding his future—a future that he wanted to share with Maya.

He'd spent his life flying in high-risk situations because he wanted to be like his father and his grandfather, but realizing he never could, he'd switched gears, planning to buy the aviation business. Except for the one last risky job that had almost cost not only his life, but Maya's and Jake's.

The problem was that Connor wasn't sure he was ready to give it up yet. Troy had hinted that he had other properties needing recovery. Not only could Connor make a lot of money, it also would keep him doing something he loved. He hoped that he'd put his past failures to rest with the Learjet recovery, despite what they'd been through.

Still, he'd lost Darrah because she couldn't handle his risk-taking. He wouldn't lose Maya for the same reason.

Forget that he didn't even *have* Maya.

Someone cleared a throat and Connor looked up to see her standing in the door. His pulse thundered in his ears.

"I was beginning to think I'd never see you again," he said. Pathetic.

Dressed in a soft blue knit top and jeans, she strolled into the room, her honey-vanilla scent wrapping around him, bringing with it memories—the good moments—from their ordeal.

Behind her, a suited man stood in the hallway. Had he accompanied Maya? As if she'd heard his silent question, she glanced over her shoulder then back to him.

"I told them I wouldn't cooperate—tell them anything about Roberto—unless they let me see you." She stepped closer to the bed, an odd mixture of grief and hope in her eyes. "I'm glad to see you're on the mend."

Her brows knitted slightly.

"Only because you're here now." Had he said too much? He sounded like a desperate man, but her words held hope, a promise of that future he wanted with her. "Are they using you to get to your father like you feared they would?"

She toyed with the strap of her purse. "That remains to be seen."

Mere inches away, he wanted to wrap his arms around her. Instead, he watched and waited.

The ball's in your court.

"I should never have said things couldn't work out between us." Maya sat on the bed, then, and took his hand in hers.

Connor held on and squeezed, breathing in her essence, savoring this moment and hoping it was the first of many. He'd hoped beyond hope that the connection they had wasn't a fantasy born of a threatening situation.

Maya stared at him with her honey almond eyes, her long dark mane framing her face. He smiled.

"Did you mean what you said? That you want me in your life? That…"

"That I'm falling in love with you? Yes. I know we haven't known each other that long, but it feels like much longer."

Her eyes lit up at his words, hope overcoming the grief he'd seen in them earlier.

"Yes. A lot happened between us in a short period of time. Because of you, I'm safe now. You're my champion."

"Champion, huh?" He'd never been anyone's hero, much less champion.

But did she love him? She hadn't exactly said that. Maybe it was too soon. Connor thought he might crash and burn again only this time for far different reasons.

"But what about love?" he asked.

She gave him that high-wattage smile that sent his spirits rocketing—he'd been trained to resist G-forces, but nothing could have prepared him to resist Maya Carpenter.

"I trust you with my heart," Maya said. "Though some would say we haven't known each other long enough, I say life is too short. I've never loved anyone like I love you."

Connor lifted both hands to her face and drew her lips to his, kissing her thoroughly and completely, and knowing this kiss was genuine and held the promise of a future.

"You're right," he whispered. "Life *is* too short."

* * * * *

Dear Reader,

Too many times we allow our past to define our future, and often those negative things we allow to define us were never within our control to begin with. That's exactly what happens to both Connor and Maya in *Treacherous Skies*.

Maya is driven by the fact she doesn't want to be her father's daughter in any form. Even though she lives her life to escape her heritage, her father's past and his mistakes find her anyway, and end up costing her. In other words, she is running for her life, paying for her father's mistakes.

Connor allows his failures to define him, though he's never really given up on his deep need to come out on top, to be a winner like his father and his grandfather.

These characters are thrown together in a pressure-cooker situation that, though it's a cliché, becomes a refining fire. Connor is now determined to win or die, and Maya is forced to embrace her heritage in order to live, and in order to be free.

Thank goodness we have a Father in heaven and when we accept Christ we become a new creation, and our past doesn't have to define us. I hope you enjoyed reading *Treacherous Skies* and I pray that you found a spiritual nugget within the pages that speaks to you.

I enjoy hearing from my readers. You can contact me through my website at www.ElizabethGoddard.com and sign up for my newsletter to receive updates.

Elizabeth Goddard

Questions for Discussion

1. Maya has spent most of her life living away from her father because of his business. Can you relate in any way, and if so, discuss the situation and how things could be different.

2. Have you ever been in a situation where someone who'd completely destroyed your trust in them asked for a chance to make amends, and if so, what did you do? Given that Maya's father asked for a chance to see her one last time, how do you think she should have handled things?

3. Some might consider that Maya going to meet her father was a huge mistake. Consider the last time you did something that seemed like a good idea at the time, but turned out to be a mistake. Discuss what you could have done differently. Considering your decision, could you have made a better decision if given another chance, or would your decision be the same based on the information you had at the time? Why or why not?

4. We all have things in our past that try to hold us back. What came to mind as you read this story? Discuss how you'd change the past, and how you would go about changing the future, despite the past.

5. With a father and a grandfather who were heroes, Connor has some big shoes to fill. Do you think he should feel so pressured to fill them? Why or why

not? Have you ever felt pressured to meet family expectations? Explain.

6. Because Connor hasn't met with success in his jobs, he's aiming for something different, something safe. Has there ever been a time in your life when you realized what you did for a living just wasn't working, and if so, how did you change things?

7. In the end, Connor realizes that he wasn't made to do things the safe way. What do you think about his decision? Do you think he did the right thing in being willing to give up risky jobs if it meant losing Maya?

8. Maya struggles to let Connor help her with things because she doesn't want to bring harm to another person, yet she needs the help he offers. Think of a time in your life when you were struggling. Did you struggle to allow others to know what was going on in your life, or struggle to trust them to help? Why or why not?

9. Since Maya's father is a Colombian drug lord, she fears that will somehow affect who she is on the inside and outside. Our mannerisms and how we think and act are most often developed through our environment, but not completely. Often, our reactions and emotions stem from genetics. How do you think Maya should have felt about her bloodline? How do you feel about yours?

10. Early on, Connor decides he would help Maya and see things through to the end, instead of allowing

her to go it alone as she insisted that she wanted to do. Do you think he did this out of his need to be a hero, to change his perception of himself? Or do you think his desire to help Maya was something more? Why or why not?

11. Connor hasn't spoken to his brother in two years because of an argument that got out of hand. What do you think of his relationship with his brothers?

12. Have you ever been in a relationship where emotions ran high and in the end, you cut your ties? Discuss what happened. Do you want to change things? Why or why not?

13. How do you feel about Reg's interference at the end of the story when he tries to dissuade Connor and Maya from continuing their relationship? Have you ever interfered like that when you thought someone couldn't see things clearly? Discuss what happened.

14. Maya knew what her father did for a living and as already discussed, that defined much of her life, but when she discovered that he'd kidnapped and murdered another man's child, she was devastated and emotionally debilitated. How would you have reacted to such news? Do you understand her reaction regarding her father? Why or why not?

15. Circumstances forced Connor and Maya together and accelerated their romantic relationship, so in a very short period of time they each realized they wanted the other in their life. Have you endured a struggle under pressure that accelerated a relation-

ship like that? Perhaps you connected with someone you otherwise would never have known, or taken the time to know very well. Discuss what happened, and how you think a stressful situation affects relationships.